Justice in Biloxi
Anatomy of a malpractice case. A Novella

By Mark Zohar

Table of Contents

A woman undergoes an operation for a small hernia of her belly button. She ends up with severe brain damage. How and why did it happen? Could it have been prevented? Was it a "natural" complication inherent to such procedure ("shit happens")? Or was the surgeon negligent ("shit should not have happened")? Should the surgeon be sued? Shouldn't the harmed patient be compensated?

The author—a veteran general surgeon and an experienced expert witness—describes the case in details, against the general background of medical malpractice litigations. The book would be of interest to all the parties involved in the drama of medical malpractice litigations: physicians, lawyers and especially potential plaintiffs—harmed patients who want to watch what takes place at the backstage of the theater.

So come and watch the legal play, meet all the actors: the plaintiff-harmed patient, the defendant-surgeon, the lawyers and expert witnesses on both sides of the isle, the Judge. Listen to the pre-trial depositions; attend the trial in Biloxi. Will justice prevail?

Part I: The Case

1

December 2015. Anyone present on this day in the Circuit Court of Harrison County of Biloxi, Mississippi would assume that the gray haired guy sitting on the witness stand must be the defendant—the sued doctor. But no—that guy, sweating on the stand, is me—an aging general surgeon, the plaintiff's expert witness.

I take a sip of water. This cannot possibly take much longer, I think. The clock on the wall indicates 4:50. He has been torturing me for almost three hours. What else could he ask?

He is the defendant's lawyer—the one defending the surgeon who has been sued for malpractice. The plaintiff—the fat black lady who is sitting on the right, down below, is staring at the void. She does not understand much of what has been said here since the morning. I know that her brain was screwed up by the defendant.

I feel broiling in this large courtroom despite the AC. The hangover that was debilitating in the morning is abating. But the headache is returning. I massage my forehead, attempting to focus my tired eyes on the short man who is approaching the witness stand. That guy has been standing, hopping and twirling in front of me since after lunch.

"Doctor, in your written expert opinion from 2013 you stated, I quote, 'I wrote and co-edited the book *Practical Emergency Abdominal Surgery* which has become an international bestseller, translated to eight languages and subsequently updated and expanded—the 4th Edition appearing in 2015.' Did you write this Doctor?" The defense lawyer looks at me, raising the document in his left hand, pointing to it with his right index finger.

"Yes, I did mention it," I admit. *What does he want to achieve with this?*

"A best seller? You called it a bestseller?" His tone is mocking, a smirk on his face.

"Well, it was and still is a surgical bestseller. Any medical book which goes into the fourth edition must be a bestseller..."

"But Doctor, who exactly has classified your book as a bestseller? Can you name a bestseller list, listing your book as such?"

Bestseller lists? What bestseller lists? Is he out of his mind? I turn to the left, where the Judge is perched way above me on his bench. He is leaning back in his high-black chair, his right hand covering his eyes. He may be napping. I look down at the plaintiff's legal team—"my team". No sound from them. They were silent since the start of my cross-examination. No help from their side.

"Sir, I don't understand your question. This is a surgical book, not a novel, you know."

"Doctor, it was you who called your own book a bestseller. Not me. So was it listed on any bestseller list, like the one of the New York Times? Or do you simply like to invent things and glorify yourself?"

"Sir, I am not aware that there are any bestseller lists of professional medical books. My book sells very well around the world, in multiple languages, so I consider it a bestseller..." I answer in tired voice.

Even before I conclude the sentence the defendant's lawyer is already back at his desk, fishing for another document. What now? What is there left to be asked?

The defense lawyer finds what he was looking for—a transparency sheet. He places it on the projector. "Your honor..." he starts.

Just be cool. This has to finish soon. He cannot go on forever. This Judge does not look as someone who would postpone dinner, let alone pre-prandial sundowners. And you, I tell myself, you will be soon jumping into the blue pool of the Casino Hotel across the road. Think about a nice drink, later at the bar. Will I see her again? The image of her luxurious, statuesque figure rushes through my mind as I try to focus my eyes on the defense lawyer and his next question. *Just be cool.*

From the start, the case seemed to me straightforward, not controversial. The ultra-brief operative report told the whole story: an obese, black woman in her 40th undergoes a laparoscopic umbilical hernia repair. The surgeon attempts to induce the pneumoperitoneum (to fill the abdomen with gas) with a *Veress* needle—that she inserts through the right upper quadrant of the abdominal wall. She then connects the needle immediately to the insufflating machine. The insufflator monitor reads, "occluded". The surgeon removes the needle, reinserts it at the same spot, and again connects it to the insufflator of CO_2. Again, it reads, "occluded". The surgeon removes the needle, checks that it is patent, and shoves it back into the same location in the right upper quadrant. This is her third attempt! She re-connects the needle to the gas machine—now the monitor immediately reads "14".

While the surgeon notices that the abdomen is not "ballooning" as expected, the anesthetist declares that the blood pressure is not recordable, and the arterial oxygen saturation is declining. A few seconds later the patient's heart stops. A CPR is conducted. The operating room fills up with up to twenty persons—anesthetists, cardiologists, intensivists, radiologists. A chest X ray is obtained to rule out a pneumothorax, drugs are given. Eventually the heart is re-started only to go into a severe arrhythmia.   After some time, an echo machine is wheeled in; it reveals air bubbles filling both sides of the heart.

Yeah! The diagnosis of air emboli is finally made. At last, the patient is place in the *Durant position* (left lateral decubitus position—lying on her left side) and somebody tries to aspirate air bubbles from the right heart through a central venous line. Meanwhile the surgeon decides to open the abdomen in order to "evacuate the pneumoperitoneum". With anoxic brain injury, the patient is moved to the ICU to start a few months of hospitalization—ending with significant neurological deficits. Brain damage. Now, she is the plaintiff sitting the whole day in the Circuit Court of Harrison County, Biloxi, the great State of Mississippi, ignored by all, comprehending nothing.

The operative report was sent to me by the patient's lawyers some three years before the trial. There was no question in my mind: I saw negligence written all over the twenty some dictated lines.

Actually, as usually is the case, I was first contacted by phone:

"Doctor, my name is Dwight Browning; I've a Law Office in New Orleans. We represent a patient who sustained brain injury after undergoing a hernia repair. I wonder if you would be interested to review this case for us."

I would receive such calls sporadically. Perhaps three or four times a year. As a rule, the calls came from out of the State— where I live and practice. They know that doctors are disinclined to testify against their local colleagues. It could ruin their career. On the other hand, finding a local expert to *defend* the sued colleague is easy.

I did not advertise myself as an expert witness; I did not solicit legal work. They would find me on *google* or *PUBMED* searches, leading to one of my publications relevant to their clients' troubles. Alternatively, they would see my books, dedicated to abdominal surgery and its complications. Why not try this guy, they would think probably.

"Yes, I'm a general surgeon and I do lots of hernia operations," I replied. "So what happened? How did your client manage to end up with a brain injury? Was there something wrong with the anesthesia? You know, I'm not an anesthetist…"

I would decline working on any case that does not fall under my specialty. I would not accept a case that, although within the scope of general surgery, has involved a procedure that I were currently not performing. Like for example, a thyroidectomy. I could imagine the defense attorney asking, "Doctor, how many thyroidectomies have you performed last year?" In brief: to accept a case and effectively support it you have to be a "real expert", with current experience in the case-specific field.

"Nothing wrong with the anesthesia," the Louisiana lawyer answered and briefly recounted the story.

"Gee, air emboli during umbilical hernia surgery, this sounds fishy," I said. "I'll need to see the whole story, to review the whole chart, everything. OK?"

"Great. And what is your fees schedule doctor"?

"I charge five hundred bucks per hour. The preliminary review like this rarely takes more than two to four hours, including some literature search. By the way, be aware that after reviewing the material I may turn the case down. That is, if I reach the opinion that the surgeon did not deviate from the standard of care. You know, things can go wrong even if the surgeon does everything according to the book. Besides, I never ever support frivolous claims or claims which I judge have little chances to be successful…"

"Yes Sir, I know, I know," the lawyer sounded as if he has to hear the same story every day, which probably was the case. "We'll be sending the material and a retainer. Two thousands sound OK?"

"Yes, thank you." Upfront the case seemed interesting and challenging. And who would object to a few thousand dollars? Taxable of course. As to the "retainer": how could I forget a case from a few years prior that I reviewed for a woman lawyer from Philadelphia. I sent her a detailed opinion on why the case of her client, who had suffered a bile leak after gallbladder surgery, does not suggest any negligence on the part of the surgeon, and thus should not be litigated. I never heard from her again. I was naïve. Not again—with lawyers, you submit your work only after you get the money.

Within a week, the patient's chart landed on my desk. The first item to be looked at—the crucial one—was the operative report. A well-conceived, well-written, detailed operative report is for the surgeon what the body camera is for the cop—the black box for the pilot. There is a caveat however: whereas the body camera or the black box record objective images, or data gathered in *real time*, the operative report is being written by the surgeon *after* the events had occurred. The surgeon can report whatever his brain tells him. He can write that he looked at all corners of the abdomen when the truth is that he had missed the pelvis; he can write that the abdomen was "dry" when he closed it, while in realty he had ignored the bleeding from the liver. He can dictate whatever. However, in general I tend to examine such reports with the assumption that they reflect what actually took place at the operation. Anyway, if they are not accurate then *res ipsa loquitor*—the thing, the complication, speaks for itself.

I was eager to see how a simple, relatively minor hernia operation could produce such a serious complication. It did not take me long to figure it out.

The patient, Katrina Gospel, was a hefty—more than two hundred pounds—black lady, in her let 40's. On March, 2013, she was taken to the operating room, where the defendant surgeon attempted a laparoscopic repair of the patient's umbilical hernia, under general anesthesia.

The surgeon wrote:

"A Veress needle was inserted within the right upper quadrant in the usual fashion at approximately the level of the anterior axillary line, the insufflation tubing was attached to the Veress needle and the reading on the monitor read occluded. The Veress needle was then removed and placed through the same puncture site and again the monitor read occluded. At this time, the Veress needle was removed and was inspected. The tubing was noted to be functional with passage of CO_2 gas. The needle was again inserted through the same puncture site. The pressure was noted to increase to 20 almost immediately, although the abdomen appeared to not insufflate, and then again read occluded…"

I sensed that it is an honest report. I imagined the surgeon sitting down in front of the Dictaphone, still distressed and traumatized—the adrenalin surging in her veins—from the unexpected disaster; trying to summarize the dramatic events in laconic, telegraphic language. Did I feel some sympathy for the surgeon? Of course. I could feel her anguish. I knew how it feels: you start a straightforward procedure, expecting it to be uneventful, and suddenly, you are fighting to save the patient's life—often not knowing from where the lightning has struck.

I read the rest of the report: "At this time, the CRNA (certified nurse anesthetist) John Jennings, noted the patient to be becoming hypotensive as well as hypoxemic. The needle was removed and the procedure aborted at this time. The patient was noted to be in asystole. Chest compressions were begun. The endotracheal tube was checked for adequate position. A chest x ray and a full lab panel were sent. Her chest X-ray was within normal limits without evidence of pneumothorax…"

I did not like the passive voice of the narrator: why not write, "I removed the needle" rather than the "needle was removed"? For God's sake: the needle was not removed by a third party. You have removed the needle—so why not say so! The longer I read the report the more it irritated me—the style, the inflexibility, the procrastination—the emerging negligence.

"A TEE (transesophageal echocardiography) was then performed and she was noted to have air within the heart, within both the right and left sides. At this time, a Swan-Ganz catheter was inserted and she was placed in the lateral decubitus position. Blood was aspirated from the ventricle and there was a copious amount of air within the aspirated blood. This was performed by Anesthesia…."

At least she is not lying, I thought. It must have taken them ages to get the TEE machine into the OR, to find somebody who knows how to use it. How many minutes it took them to diagnose the air emboli and attempt to treat it?

"At that time, I elected to assure that the abdomen was completely desufflated. An upper midline incision was made using a 15 scalpel scalpel…"

Stupid. Why open the abdomen? Who cares about the size of scalpel?

"The subcutaneous tissue was divided. The fascia identified. The fascia was open. The peritoneum was divided and the abdominal cavity entered…"

Now she is chattering away, I thought. She told us already that the abdomen was opened. Don't we know that in order to open it one has to divide all the layers?

"There was no rush of air or blood evacuated from the abdominal cavity."

Surprise, surprise. Did you really expected a "rush" of anything?

This was going through my mind when I read the operative report:

Yes, I prefer open umbilical hernia repairs to the laparoscopic ones. I can do it under local anesthesia rather the general anesthesia required for the laparoscopic procedure—why convert a "little" operation into a "big" one? And yes, I favor an open access for pneumoperitoneum over the Veress needle: like many other surgeons I want to be sure that from the start I pump the gas into the peritoneal cavity and not into other structures. Nevertheless, I acknowledge that there are many ways to skin a cat—some great surgeons prefer the Veress needle.

However, I had a problem with a surgeon inserting the Veress needle into the right upper quadrant, where a fatty, enlarged liver could lie just underneath. I had a problem with the surgeon's stubborn doggedness of re-inserting the needle at the same place (three times!)—without obtaining any of the available maneuvers (not even one!) which could document that the needle is in the right space—before connecting it to the gas-pumping machine. I had a problem with not inserting the needle at the *Palmer point* (in the left upper quadrant), which is considered safer because the absence of underlying solid organs or large blood vessels. I had a problem with not using an open access—if not at the initial attempt then at the second or third time. I had a problem with not removing the needle immediately after the monitor read "20"—a reading suggesting that the needle has been placed where it should not have been—into the liver or a large vein. I had a problem with the surgeon not realizing immediately that the patient's collapse was, most likely, caused by gas emboli and thus not placing the patient in the life saving (and brain saving in this case) *Durant position*—in order to unlock the

obstructing air lock which was blocking the outflow of the right
ventricle of the heart. Finally, I had a problem with the surgeon
performing an unnecessary laparotomy in this critically ill patient
to "decompress" (the non-existing) pneumoperitoneum. Didn't
she remember that no gas has been insufflated into the abdominal
cavity?

At that time, I did not seek any information about the
surgeon. I was aware that the surgeon was a woman; the name on
the report was Katlyn Conway. The google search had to be
deferred until I reach my opinion. I wanted to be detached and
impartial. My chore was to decide whether the surgeon had
breached her professional duty to the patient; that is, did she
deviate from the "standard of care". A term that means what an
average surgeon is expected to do under similar circumstances,
providing similar resources are available to her. The "average"
refers to an average surgeon licensed and practicing in the USA—
not Russia; while the term "similar circumstances" implies an
operating room in an average American hospital—not some
mission hospital in the depth of the African jungle. The other
elements of malpractice litigation had to be considered as well:
did *damages* occur because of the breach? Was there a direct
causation between the *breach* and *damages*? However, if the
standard of care has not been breached then there is no point to
proceed with the litigation.

5

I had no doubts: the surgeon on this case deviated from the standard of care. Such disaster would have not happened, should have not occurred, in the hands of an average, prudent surgeon. My opinion was: our lady surgeon was negligent.

At the same time, I had to recognize that the standard of care is easily stretched like chewing gum. What I consider "negligence" may be portrayed by the opposing expert witness as "bad luck—despite exemplary conduct by a competent surgeon." Thus, before concluding my opinion I presented the case (names, hospital, location—not mentioned) to a large group of surgeons subscribed to an online discussion group. I described the case and asked:

The patient survived but suffered severe brain damage. Your verdict please:
1. Shit happens.
2. Shit could have been prevented.
3. Shit should have been prevented.
4. Shit represents negligence.

None of the many surgeons who replied chose the first answer. Instead, all picked the last two. They wrote:

"I didn't know anyone inserts a Veress needle into the right upper quadrant. Palmer's point is in the left upper quadrant. The surgeon went into the renal vein or the inferior cava or something. I would think he was following some non-standard technique that led to this."

"Shit could and should have been prevented. Three attempts at insufflation and every time at high pressure should have alerted the surgeon. He could have also used the Palmer test before insufflation. This complication happened to me once and it was immediately recognized. The patient survived without sequelae."

"RUQ is not considered a "safe" place, as opposed to Palmer's point in the LUQ. Repeating the failed attempt 3 times is wrong. His shit represents negligence."

"I am thinking the surgeon may have crossed the negligence line, in doing the same thing three times, and not doing something different to verify proper needle location."

"Well, it makes me glad that I don't even think about doing a lap repair for an umbilical hernia. Direct open repair for me."

"It seems the surgeon didn't think logically. Machine said that needle 'occluded' twice. The needle was checked and was patent. So the third attempt was wrong."

"I perform all my laparoscopies with open access technique. You might still have visceral injuries but I presume there is zero risk of intra vascular insufflation. I cannot understand why the surgeon didn't change the site of insufflation or switched to open technique."

"As the monitor read 'occluded', I suppose intra vascular insufflation of gas occurred

"I don't understand the need for upper midline laparotomy."

"Negligence."

"Guilty on all last three charges."

"To answer your specific query this case represents negligence. But to elaborate without being judgmental: 1. I do not do repair umbilical hernia by laparoscopy and do not see any advantage of doing so—there are only disadvantages. 2. For many years, I avoid using the Veress needle and enter the abdomen by open method. However senior or expert, the laparoscopic surgeon should always be careful of the first entry into abdomen, whether with Veress or by open method."

"The RUQ Veress access could perhaps be argued but the rest of the operation not. In retrospect, there was ample warning of misplacement and I do not see how this could be defended. Once sure, twice perhaps, thrice is the vice, and hence arguably negligent. I was taught and try to teach that a second failure of any surgical step needs a re-think and alteration in process."

"Surely indefensible?"

"It's the Einsteinian definition of lunacy. Doing the same thing over and over, each time expecting a different outcome."

Now, with not even one surgeon out of a few hundred offering a dissenting viewpoint, namely, that what happened to this patient does not necessarily mean "negligence"; with no one coming out to "defend" the surgeon, to suggest potential mitigating factors to reduce her culpability, I was left with no qualms.

I called Mr. Browning's Law Firm in New Orleans with my opinion: Negligence. I am ready to support the lawsuit against the surgeon.

6

Eau Claire, Wisconsin, June 2015. It was the morning of an early summer day in Wisconsin, cool but sunny. She stepped out of the airport taxi. I had just parked my F-105 after an hour drive southwards through the North woods.

We shook hands and greeted each other.

The first thing she said was: "Oh', it's lovely up here, so cool and dry. Like, from a sauna to an air-conditioned room! I've never been up north before."

"Yes, I know what you mean. I remember Miami in the summer—I bet Mississippi and Louisiana are not better."

I had already seen her smiling face on her office's webpage. Now I could assess the rest: tallish, heavy set verging on chubby, wrapped in a formal dark suit over a white silk shirt. She walked, rather wobbly, on black high heels. *Why do they have to wear such heels*? To pose an image of authority and command in men-dominated field? Didn't that lawyer—what was her name? — who managed to acquit me of a malpractice lawsuit in a courtroom in Iowa, some eight years earlier, wore five-inch stilettoes as well?

The lawyer stepping out of the taxi was Veronica Chapman. She was the junior partner for Dwight Browning. From her webpage, I had already learned that she had received her BA in a Mississippi University, graduated from a Law School at the same State, followed by the usual years of internships in the State bureaucracy, working for some Judge. Now, I gathered, she has to be at her early or mid-thirties, a beginner at the private law firm, and a novice in the field of medical malpractice.

My immediate reaction to Veronica was positive: she was soft spoken, polite, humbly mannered and genial. *A nice lawyer for a change.*

There is, I believe, some truth in what Anton Chekhov wrote, "Surgeons are just the same as lawyers; the only difference is that lawyers merely rob you, whereas surgeons rob you and kill you too" (he used the term "doctors" rather than "surgeons"). But in reality, the two professions cannot be more different from each other. We surgeons fight in the operative trenches, dripping blood, swimming virtually in urine and feces; we surgeons have to decide instantly on matters of life and death—we take risks and learn to live with unending uncertainties. This affects our personalities. We tend to be spontaneous, outspoken, sardonic verging on sarcastic; some of us enjoy black humor. These defense mechanisms helping us to cope. Lawyers, as we all know, are an entirely different breed. They fight their wars in the deposition rooms and courts; they swim not in shit but in paper; they are coated not in blood but in endless verbiage. They are not spontaneous but calculated. They do not decide on matters of life and death but on the dollar value of the latter. It takes us thirty seconds to decide to do something; it takes them a few years to show that what we did in these few seconds was wrong. The only item that unites us, surgeons and lawyers, is the quest for the dollar and some professional pride. Otherwise, we are so unlike and, obviously, we do not share love for each other.

Nevertheless, we need each other. According to a 2011 study published in the *New England Journal of Medicine*, across specialties, 7.4% of physicians annually had a malpractice claim against them; 1.6% made an indemnity payment. For surgeons the risk of being sued is more significant: 15% of general surgeons were involved in a malpractice claim—4% made a payment. The "cumulative career malpractice risk" is much higher: 80% of physicians in surgical specialties (including general surgery) and 74% of physicians in obstetrics and gynecology were projected to face a claim by the age of 45 years. Whereas by the age of 65 years, 99% of those in high-risk (e.g. surgical) specialties were projected to face a claim. The projected career risk of making an indemnity payment was 71% for surgeons by the age of 65.

With such great legal risks, we surgeons need lawyers. We depend on them; we are exposed to them from the early phases of our careers. Who else can help navigate us through the obscure legal world, defending us from what we usually perceive—rightly or wrongly—as frivolous, groundless or unjustified accusations?

Alas, it is a symbiotic relationship: layers need us too. They either sue us or defend us; this is how they make their living. Often they change sides: at the beginning of their career, they would work for an insurance company and gather experience in defending alleged medical offenders. Once they have learned all the tricks of the trade they would go private and sue the doctors they had previously defended. On one side of the isle, they try to prove that all lawsuits are frivolous—all surgeons did what is right, and all expert witnesses supporting the plaintiffs are clueless or unqualified hired guns. However, once they change sides they adopt the opposite narrative: suddenly the surgeon is the enemy, the client has been harmed, and the expert witness is essential to achieve victory, namely money for them; yes also for their client. No wonder then that surgeons perceive lawyers as parasites, greedy parasites; like blood sucking maggots thriving on wounds. Even such maggots or leeches can be beneficial— they can be used to clean infected wounds and protect you from a lawsuit.

When a lawyer saves you from a lawsuit he is a hero, when he wins the case for the plaintiff and you are found guilty—he becomes a despised enemy.

Now, when I met with Veronica I was neutral. I liked what I saw. I felt we could work well together, even though, from the start, I sensed her greenness. But let me regress a little before we enter the deposition room…

7

Sun Tzu wrote, "Wheels of justice grind slow but grind fine". I query how "fine" the wheels of justice grind but we know how slow it can be. When Veronica Chapman called me almost two years after I had been contacted by her boss, the case has gone missing from my memory.

"Which case? You say you are from Mississippi?" I hesitated, searching my mind.

"Doctor, you have written an opinion for us. You signed an affidavit enabling the lawsuit against the surgeon and her hospital."

"Oh, yes, the lap hernia, the air emboli, a lady surgeon, yes, now it rings a bell. An interesting case. Mississippi? I thought it was North Carolina. So how can I help you now?"

"Well doctor, I'm calling to schedule a deposition. That is, the defendants' lawyers want to depose you. Once we agree on the site and date, I will be sending you additional material. This will include copies of our deposition of the surgeon and the defense's deposition of the plaintiff. OK?"

"OK. Who'll be paying me for the deposition?"

"The defense," she said. "Obviously, you can continue billing us for the time you spend on the preparation. What are your fees?"

"Still five hundred per hour. I will be charging for travel time as well." I knew the usual terms of the deal. The side requesting the deposition pays the deposed experts. The plaintiff's lawyers pay out of their pockets for deposing the opposing experts. The defense is well funded by the deep pockets of insurance companies or self-insured hospitals—they pay not only the opposing experts but also the defense lawyers for their time. That is why the plaintiff's lawyers tend to depose very sparingly. That is also, why defense lawyers tend to depose "everybody"— the more they depose—the longer the case is allowed to drag on— the more money for them.

A week later, I received this:

IN THE CIRCUIT COUT OF HARRISON COUNTY

KATRINA GOSPEL
    PLAINTIFF

VS.   CIVIL ACTION NUMBER: B3320-17-51

The ADVENTIST MEDICAL CENTER AT GULFPORT
      DEFENDANTS   AND KATLYN CONWAY,
M.D

                NOTICE FOR DEPOSITION FOR DR.
MARK ZOHAR

Please take notice that the Defendants, The Adventist Medical Center at Gulfport and Dr. Katlyn Conway, will take the testimony on oral and/or video examination of Dr. Mark Zohar before a court reporter on Monday, the 29th day of June.

A video? I was not surprised. This has become a routine: the defense video filming the opposing experts, litigating lawyers filming the defendants. Everybody videotapes each other. Like a filming class in a community college.

"The video deposition of the opposing party is one of the many weapons in your trial arsenal," I read in one of those how-to-do manuals for lawyers. "Expecting to play the video for your jury will help you to formulate your questions; will force you to better stage and produce the deposition. At the end of the day, the deposition is theater too…" *Yes, theatre, this is how lawyers think*. Besides, the video may help the opposing legal team to "study the expert"—how does he answer the questions? What his body language is like—would the jury like him? What irritates him? What are his weak points? How can we get under his skin—to diminish his stature and distort his demeanor in front the jury and judge? In sum: how can we KILL him?

Quite possible, I thought, the video recording would be viewed by one of those "court room psychologists, or "speech and body language consultants". Defense lawyers with deep pockets often hire such "experts"; not only to coach the defendant and the defense's experts on how to conduct themselves in court but also to assess the opposing expert—how convincing he will appear? Should we take the risk to go all the way to court? Or should we settle? *Yes, it's a theatre.*

At the bottom of the document, I found who would be the main defense lawyer on this case—the one who will depose me. His name: Francis Z. Furrer, III. Who is he? A quick Google search provided the basic facts: At his late 50's, born in Biloxi, Mississippi, college and Law School in Mississippi—he was the managing editor of the school's "Law Review". Gee, I was thinking, this is exactly what Obama did at Harvard Law School. A stint in Washington DC, working for a Mississippi Republican Senator. Next, as usual, a few years clerking for some local Judges. His current Law Office situated in Gulfport. *Good ol' Southern Boy*, I thought, a great C.V—a strong asset to litigated hospital and that lady surgeon.

I studied at leisure the entire hospital chart of the patient— the plaintiff. The surgeon's operative report was the "smoking gun" but I had to dissect the whole chart for the ammunition used to fire the gun—more ammunition that I could use against the defendants.

Reading modern hospital charts is an excruciating process. In the pre-electronic days, it was hard enough to try to decipher the notoriously illegible hand scribble of so many doctors. At least one could assess, more or less, their though process—what were they thinking and how did they justify their actions. This was often nicely captured by the transcribed dictations. These days, however, increasingly, the charts are produced by elaborated commercial software. For a single page of valuable information, you need to shift through a hundred pages of non-significant data. To fish out a lentil size of gold you need to skim through tons of electronic gibberish.

The copy of Mrs. Katrina Gospel's chart from the Adventist Medical Center at Gulfport weighted only a few pounds. To start with, I was interested to find out more about the umbilical hernia. In her operative report, the surgeon provided no details about the size of the hernia, and whether it was symptomatic. Obviously, not all asymptomatic hernias need to be repaired.

I discovered that Katrina had been seen by Dr. Conway already in 2012—some seven months before the disastrous operation. The reason stated for the encounter was a *lipoma*—a small fatty tumor situated under the skin, just below the patient's left shoulder blade. The surgeon then removed the tumor in the operating room under local anesthesia and i.v sedation. I read the surgeon's pre-operative notes, including physical examination. "Abdomen normal" it said. *So where is the hernia?*

Did it suddenly pop up during the few months interval between the removal of the lipoma and the hernia operation? Or, more likely, the "abdomen normal" statement means nothing. "Modern" doctors are not as thorough in their physical examination as the older generation. The surgeon may not have examined the abdomen at all at that time. Why should she? The patient's problem was the fatty lump—why bother with the abdomen? The "abdomen-normal" is a "copy-paste" product. Commonly, doctors copy/paste whole templates—entire pre-conceived paragraphs of texts—into the document of encounter. With a single click, one can insert a report of "a completely normal physical examination". It saves time and allows charging higher rates for the encounter. The more "items" included in the reported examination—the more "complex" the case appears to be—it can be billed higher. This represents an ongoing fraud—a fraud so entrenched in the system that it has become a norm.

The rest of the chart did not add much to my case against the surgeon. I read about the events occurring after the botched operation. The prolonged stay in the intensive care, the neurological consults documenting brain damage, the slow but incomplete recovery, and the attempts of rehabilitation. This however was outside my scope. The plaintiff's legal team, I was sure, will hire a neurologist to testify about the damage incurred to Katrina's brain. I was equally sure that the defense would bring up an army of "experts" to "prove" that the patient's brain had been flawed even before the operation.

Just at the bottom of the pile, I found a sheet from the Surgical Clinic: a few weeks after the botched operation Katrina was wheeled to the Clinic to see her surgeon. The surgeon noted, "a well healed midline upper abdominal wound. Further follow up with primary care provider. I do no need to see her again." No word about anything else. Nothing about the patient's mental status. I smiled to myself: she could have written "uneventful postoperative course." I thought about the "surgical ostrich syndrome"—the surgeon living in denial like an ostrich burying his head in the sand.

Next I dwelt into the deposition of the patient—the plaintiff herself. She had been deposed (on video as well) just a few months prior, the hundred and eight single-side, double spaced, printed pages of the transcription did not take more than half an hour to skim over. I predicted that I would not be finding much of value here as the purpose of the defense in such cases is clear—to show how unreliable the plaintiff was and still is; and, in our case, to suggest that her brain had been touched even before the air emboli had lodged in it.

"Counsels may now introduce themselves for the record," says the court reporter.

"Francis Furrer; I represent the Adventist Medical Center at Gulfport and Dr. Katlyn Conway."

"And I'm Veronica Chapman, and I represent Katrina Gospel."

After the court reporter swears in the witness, Mr. Furrer starts to examine her.

"Mrs. Gospel, my name is Francis Furrer. We met just a couple of minutes ago. And I'm just going to be asking you some questions today, all right?"

"Uh-huh", the witness says.

"And one of the things we have to remind you to do is to answer 'yes' and 'no', not 'uh-huh' and 'huh-huh', okay?"

"Uh-huh", answers Katrina.

"Can you say 'yes'?

It would have been interesting to watch the video recording, I thought—did the black woman manage to irritate our gentleman of coastal Mississippi?

"Yes", Katrina replies.

"All right. So I—I'm not trying to pick on you, but we have to remind people to do that all the time."

Like talking to a baby.

And so it plodded on. Questions about her birth place ("California"), about her previous addresses ("I do not remember"), about her children, her previous jobs, her education (she did not finish high school), about her psychiatric ,medications ("I'm bipolar, don't remember which medications"), about her current partner ("he buys shrimp of the boat and sells it"), about an injury to her leg following which she had applied for disability, about the last job she had ("home care provider"). So it trudged on until, on page 42, Mr. Furrer stumbled on something of interest:

"Have—have you ever been charged with any kind of crime?" the defense lawyer asks.
"Yes".
"Okay. So how—what was the crime that you served time for?"
"Possession of a controlled substance."
"What was the controlled substance?"
"Crack cocaine."
"So you were charged with possession of crack cocaine, and then you had to serve some time because of that"?
"Right", the black woman admits.
"So you were charged with a crime, right"?
"Right."
"Okay. And I assume you were arrested because of that?"
"Yes."
"And then how much time did you serve?"
"About two weeks."
"Two weeks?"
What a *nudnik*, I was thinking. Did he want her to serve life term on a chain gang in Mississippi?
"Yep," the woman replies.
"And that was in California?"
"Right."
"And was that in a county jail?"
"Yes."

And now, the lawyer draws out a confession that the plaintiff had been using cocaine for twenty years; that she has been "clean" for the last six years but, alas, she smoked cigarettes until that last operation. "How much?" he asks.
"About a pack-and-a-half a day". No, she does not drink now but did in the past. What? "Tequila".
Next, the defense lawyer addresses the patient's past medical history. Seven pregnancies. Doctors. Hospitals. Her mental diseases. Medications.

Finally, on page 61 of the transcript, Mr. Furrer arrives at the point of interest:

"Now, the case that we're here to talk about is a case against Adventist Medical Center and Dr. Conway. And you know Dr. Conway to be a surgeon there at the hospital, don't you?"

"Uh-huh."

"Yes?"

"Yes."

"Can you tell me the first time you remember going to Adventist Medical Center at Gulfport for any reason?"

"Yes, I was there before…I had a tumor on my back and I was there to get it removed, and Dr. Conway was the doctor to do the surgery…she told me she had to do the surgery to see if it was a …a cancerous tumor. So that's what she did. And it came back it wasn't…it was non-cancerous. It was a fatty lump. But yes, she had it removed."

Bull, I thought. A lipoma on the back feels like a lipoma. No need to exclude cancer. No need to scare the patient with cancer.

"And there weren't any problems with the operation, were there?" asks Mr. Furrer.

"There were, I had to go to the ER to get it drained because it pused up. It was a lot of pus."

"And then you went back to see Dr. Conway, right? For what?"

"For my naval. I kept going to her until the wound on my back healed and then, then she seen my belly button, and, and she said she could fix that, so I decided to have the surgery to fix my naval."

So typical, I thought. The obese patient had an asymptomatic lipoma removed from her back—followed by complications. Next, she is being procured for yet another unnecessary operation. The fat lady was living with that hernia for years. What is the rush to repair it? It is the money! The constant pressure on the surgeon to justify her generous salary. The hospital wants you to produce!

"So did you talk with Dr. Conway about what that surgery was going to be?" asks the lawyer.

"Yes."

"And she told you what procedures she was going to follow?"

Yes."

"And what do you recall she told you?"

"She told me that you can have it—one way would be with less scarring—or I could have it another way and I would still have a scar. So I decided to have the surgery that had the less scarring."

This is why I enjoy reading transcripts of depositions, I thought. It is like a perfect dialogue by a talented novelist. This must be how the surgeon convinced the patient to choose the laparoscopic procedure over the open one. Anyone would choose the operation associated with (alleged) "less scarring" if the risks and outcome were equivalent.

"And do you recall if she called that a laparoscopic procedure?" asks the defense lawyer.

"No."

"Okay. Do you recall what she did call it?"

"No."

She does not need to be brain damaged not to remember, I thought. Almost half of patients cannot recall details from a recent encounter with their doctor. Many cannot recall his or her name.

Next, the lawyer, after confirming with the patient that her husband had been present during that encounter, shows a few documents—marked as Exhibits—representing the forms of "informed consent" for the anesthesia and operation. He points to the signatures on those forms and asks the witness to confirm that these were signed by her.

"Uh-huh."

"Now, you would have signed these documents when you checked into the hospital; is that right?"

"Right."

"And do you recall anyone going over the documents with you at all?"

"No."

Of course, she does not remember. These days, on the morn of the operation, they make you sign a thousand forms. Financial, medical, nursing. Sign here, sign there. Small print, densely printed pages, you cannot see anything without your reading glasses. You cannot read English. You are stressed and scared.

Just sign here. And you do. More fodder to our lip service and the booming bureaucracy.

The lawyer continues: "When you met with Dr. Conway in her office and talked about the surgery, did—did she talk to you at all about the risks and benefits of the surgery?"

"Yeah."

"All right. What do you recall about that?"

"Just, generally, she spoke about risks."

"You don't have any specific memory of it?"

"No."

On further interrogation, the plaintiff says that she has no memory at all of the hospital stay during the early weeks after the operation. She remembers however being in the rehabilitation section of the hospital.

The lawyer: "During that period of time, do you remember having any conversation with Dr. Conway?"

"No. I've seen her couple of times going through the hallway. That was about it. She never came to my room or anything."

"You—you don't remember her ever coming to your room?"

"No."

"You—you don't remember having any conversation with her?"

"Nope."

"Have you—have you ever had any conversation with Dr. Conway since the time of your surgery?"

"Nope."

Oh', I thought, the surgeon committed a huge mistake—she had abandoned the patient. Abandoning your complicated patient to his or her fate breeds bitterness, hate and desire for revenge. The bigger the complication, the more significant its consequences, the more intensive should be the surgeon's personal commitment to the management of the patient. Oh, sure, we know how unpleasant and stressful is to watch the disasters of our own botched operation. One may think, "the residents can look after him, the internist can better deal with the problem…they don't need my daily involvement…". But the family and patient will think otherwise: "that frickin' surgeon, he fucked up so badly and now he has lost interest. But he took the money, the SOB!"   I would refer this young surgeon, I thought, to the book *"Common sense prevention and management of surgical complications"* and make her read this:

"Advice: see the complicated patient as often as you can, stop by when you walk by her room, touch her, and chat with the family. Even if her condition is desperate and she is busy dying, even if she has been transferred to a different ward or another hospital—keep in touch and show interest! People want to be respected until the end."

Slowly, an early opinion of this surgeon emerged in my mind. I continued reading.

After a few pages of chitchat about Katrina's children Mr. Furrer returns to the same point: "Now, let me go back to asking you about Dr. Conway. So you have never had a conservation that you recall with Dr. Conway?"

"No."

"Are you mad with Dr. Conway?"

"No."

"Are you upset with her?"

"I'm upset."

"Okay. And why—why are you upset?"

"Because of what happened to me."

The remaining thirty something pages of the deposition focused on Katrina's residual disabilities. I skimmed through it. My role in the case did not include assessment of the severity of the residual damages caused by the operative injury. My job was to show that the injury could and would have been prevented by a more cautious surgeon—one who adheres to the standard of care.

8

Who exactly is that Dr. Conway? I had already read her operative report. I looked at her scanty notes in the patient's chart. I knew just a little what Katrina, the patient, felt about her: she was not "mad" with the surgeon but only "upset."

So I googled up Dr. Conway. Her CV popped up immediately on the webpage of the Adventist Medical Center at Gulfport. "Birth October 5, 1972", it said. This made her forty-three years old. A great age to be a surgeon, I thought—she is more than ten years after having completed residency, having gained some experience and independence, but still in possession of a young physiology. True, not wholly mature yet—this should arrive at her early 50's (or never) —but near the top of her technical skills. I remembered myself at that age—that was when I arrived in this country. Aggressive, arrogant, confident that with my knowledge and experience and operative skills I can cut on anything.

Dr. Conway's headshot on the webpage, probably taken ten year ago: a smiling young woman, shoulder-long brown hair, parted on the left, far cry from stylish. Not what one would call a pretty girl. But pleasant: a white, friendly smile, a slightly curved nose, well fed cheeks. Medical School—Louisiana State University. Surgical residency—a large Clinic in New Orleans. Then a year in some private surgical group in rural North Carolina. Then back south as an associate professor in a Louisiana academic center. Last nine years at the Adventist Medical Center at Gulfport. Five listed publication as a second and third author. In sum, I thought, a locally trained Southern girl, who has never ventured beyond the Deep South; with no significant academic background. A typical "community surgeon"—like the majority of surgeons all over the country. Some superb, most average, some problematic.

I could imagine being in Dr. Conway's shoes. I knew the feeling of being sued by a patient. The sense of betrayal—*didn't I do my best for him*? The sense of anxiety and anguish involved in losing control, having to depend on lawyers. The sense of frustration with repeated meetings with lawyers, depositions, dragging for years and wasting your time. The sense of shame sitting in court: you—the top local surgeon—now the "accused".

The sense of depression after having lost the case. Sure, the money paid to the winning plaintiff does not come from your own pocket but you continue to hurt. Your name will be listed in "The National Practitioners Data Bank". From now on, wherever you go, wherever you apply for a job, you will be asked: "Doctor, please explain your lawsuit in Mississippi, 2015. It has been settled for a million dollars. Right?" Any case that you lose, or is settled in favor of the plaintiff, is like a permanent tattoo mark on your career. Even this is not the end of the story. Next your local State Medical Board—the State's licensing body—wakes up after receiving news of the outcome of your legal case, and starts its own investigation. More letters, more questions, and more potential adverse consequences—again reported to the National Practitioners Data Bank. If you are licensed in a few States, each State Board can initiate its own investigation. It all starts with a little lawsuit, it can drag for years, it can continue hassle you even longer, and it could blemish you forever. So you better try to win. Or even better—do not get sued!

I could place myself in Dr. Conway's shoes because I had been in her shoes before. I had been sued a few times during the 35 years of my surgical practice. I settled the first case, I won the second and I settled the third; in fact, it was settled against my will. For sometimes, the insurance company prefers to settle rather than risk a pricey loss in court. They decide to settle and you are tattooed.

I also could envisage in my mind the operating room in Gulfport, one morning two years ago. The surgeon, gowned and gloved, a lock of brown hair protruding from below her green scrub hat. She is relaxed and confident, chatting with the anesthetist while the nurses are busy arranging the laparoscopic paraphernalia. This is a routine operation; she had done numerous laparoscopic repairs of abdominal wall hernias before. *Another minor case.* She can do it with closed eyes. What is she thinking about when the scrub nurse hands her the scalpel? About the fat black belly looking up at her? About another patient admitted this morning through the ER to be seen after this operation? About her son's birthday party? Does she have any kids?   Next, she places a tiny skin incision in the right upper quadrant. The nurse hands her the Veress needle that she holds between her thumb and index finger, she inserts perpendicularly into the incision and through the abdominal wall. Does she lift the abdominal wall at the insertion site as recommended by some? Does she check that the needle is patent and the spring-loaded safety mechanism is functioning properly as mentioned in numerous surgical manuals? Does she feel the "give with a click" which is usually felt as the needle's spring mechanism crosses the posterior layer of the abdominal wall and enters the peritoneal cavity? Does she attempt any of the simple tests to verify the correct position of the needle? Probably not, otherwise she would have mentioned it in her op note.

A minute or two are passing. The surgeon attaches the insufflation tubing that connects the insufflating machine to the Veress needle—we do not know at what flow rate—and the monitor reads "occluded". *Shit, the stupid needle must be in the muscle or the pre-peritoneal fat, why are they all so bloody fat,* the surgeon perhaps is thinking. Habitually she jerks out the needle and re-inserts it at the same spot. "Occluded". Again. *Shit. Is the needle blocked by some junk—fat or something? "Could you please flush the needle," the surgeon probably tells the scrub nurse. At the same time, she must be checking whether the gas tubing is not kinked.

Now, after documenting that the gas is freely flowing though the needle, she re-introduces the needle into the abdomen, again through the same hole, and starts to pump in the CO_2. After a few seconds, she looks at the monitor. It reads "20 mm Hg". *Hell, where am I? This is much too high.* She looks at the abdomen, she taps on it with her open hands—it is not filling up with gas. *Where is this gas going?* Another few seconds and the insufflator's monitor reads "occluded". *Again. Fuck.* Is she really using the F words? Surgeons often do. I do. It comes out instinctively. A few more seconds. *What now?* she is probably thinking, until John, the nurse-anesthetist, squeaks from over the screen: "Hey, Dr. Conway, blood pressure is down, I can't read it. Shoot, O_2 sat is dropping. What's the ....". Now everybody is glued to the anesthesia monitors—watching the blood pressure and oxygen saturation figures. No one moves. Silence. Suddenly the line on the EKG monitor becomes flat. "Asystole. Start CPR", barks the nurse anesthetist, "Code blue, code blue, get help." The surgeon removes the Veress needle from the patient's abdomen and steps aside. The room fills up with anesthetists, internists, and cardiologists. She is letting them take over. Does she realize what has just happened? Does she think about air emboli? Does she know the specific emergency steps to be taken in such situation in order to improve patient's physiology? Probably at this stage, she is paralyzed, frozen. It all started as a minor, 45 minutes operation. Now this nightmare.

Dr. Conway, I thought, is not exactly the surgical equivalent of 'Sully" Sullenberger. She had functioned like an automaton. Needle in, needle out, needle in. And then she froze. As if Sully would have switch on the autopilot after his airliner's engines died. If Sully acted like Dr. Conway, his A320 with all 155 souls aboard would have been lost over the Hudson River. No, I did not expect her to be a surgical equivalent of Sully. But she could have and should have avoided having found herself in this desperate situation. *The shit could have been prevented.*

9

Would I have done better than Dr. Conway, I asked myself. Probably. Anyway, I was convinced that the way I practice surgery would have never lead to such a complication. However, like most surgeons, my own past is not free from disasters. A popular surgical aphorism maintains, "Every surgeon carries about him a little cemetery" Including myself—I have my own graveyard. The memory of the patients I helped to dispatch to the other world, by inexperience or by negligence, are clearly etched in my mind.

Early morning in a Johannesburg intensive care unit. A middle aged businessman, fresh blood pouring out his esophageal varices, like from a tap. His pretty wife by his side. Two nurses holding the bucket full of blood. I am the resident on call, unable to insert the esophagus balloon that would have stemmed the bleeding. I try and try, and he is bleeding to death. I should call for help. But I don't. I am paralyzed. Like Dr. Conway.

And what about the middle aged Russian immigrant in Israel: I, already an attending surgeon, am assisting a resident. We are removing a recurrent cancer from the remnant of his stomach. We come across a small-looking artery pumping within the dense block of scar tissue.

"Just divide it", I tell the resident.

He obeys. This is how the patient is losing his superior mesenteric artery; and thus his entire intestine turns black; within a few days, he is losing his life. Negligence.

A few years later in Brooklyn. A charming old African American bachelor who presents with rectal bleeding. I feel a mass on rectal examination. I take a rigid rectoscope, shove it up his rectum and biopsy the mass with a large forceps. The next morning his tummy is full of feces. It takes me a few months and multiple operations to save his life—leaving him with a permanent colostomy. Negligence? Yes, of course. However, the old man—I remember him being fond of Broadway musicals— had never sued me. Most harmed patients all over the world never sue—they or their surviving families are never compensated.

Like the majority of surgeons in this country, I have my own litigation history. Having had to describe at any job or license application, having had to detail it at any deposition, I could recite by heart. First, there was that black woman in Brooklyn who needed a diverting colostomy because of her large anal cancer. I was assisting a resident. Unintentionally, of course, I helped him to bring up the wrong side of the colon to the skin level. What it means is that we close-sutured the upper end of the colon, thus producing a complete colonic obstruction; we matured to the skin the lower-"dead end" of the colon—the one which produces nothing. Clear negligence! I remember seeing the patient together with the resident on the first and second day after the operation.

"Are you passing gas"? We asked.

"Yes, I am, she answered.

"Are you farting?" we asked, wanting to be sure.

"Yes, I am."

But she was not really farting. Instead, she was getting progressively bloated. Her colon was obstructed. We missed it for a few days. Then it was too late. Eventually she passed away. I remember her young, intelligent looking daughter, whom I used to update about her mother's condition. She was the one who sued the hospital and me. I admitted my error. There was no way we could have defended such a clear technical error. The case had been settled for almost a million dollars.

Another case against me was settled for approximately a similar sum. I removed a typical small sebaceous cyst from the cheek of a middle-aged man. I did not send it for pathological examination. At that time, I did not submit to pathology every piece of tissue removed. Why waste the patient's money on costly pathological assessment when the lesion removed is typically benign—like a sebaceous cyst. Two years later the patient presented elsewhere with a large skin cancer on his cheek—invading his eye socket, and needing extensive surgery. Now he had sued me for "missing" the "original" skin cancer, calling it sebaceous cyst—this is what he was told by his new surgeon. I wanted to dispute the patient's claims and oppose the lawsuit: Where was he for more than two years—why he ever returned for his scheduled follow-up? How come he was seen by other doctors during the intervening years and no one has mentioned any new lesion growing on his face? I wanted to claim that the skin cancer had nothing to do with the benign lesion that I had removed; that it was a new, rapidly growing invasive cancer.

And, most importantly, that the literature does not support routine pathological examination for each and every piece of tissue removed by a surgeon. My defense lawyer listened carefully, but after consulting a few potential expert witnesses advised the insurance company to settle the case. The experts' opinion was that the "prevailing practice around here is to send everything to pathology." I had lost. Yet again, my "crime" had been reported to the National Practitioner Data Bank. The State Board disciplined me, mandating that I take special education in "cutaneous cancer surgery". My employers—the party paying for the settlement—demanded that from then on I submit *each and every piece of tissue removed for pathological examination*; and that I photograph everything I cut off. Since then I have religiously adhered to such "defensive" practice. *Who cares about the cost to the patient and the society, it is not our money— all what we want is not to be sued!*

However, the most "traumatic" malpractice case filed against took place when I had been practicing in rural Iowa.

10

It is February 2008 in Fort Madison. A quaint little town in Southern Iowa, on the banks of the Mississippi. The mighty river is frozen. After a long week in court, being accused of negligence and malpractice, one would want to forget the nightmare—to leave it behind. However, most surgeons would remember it forever.

It is the fourth day of the trial. We are listening to the closing arguments by the plaintiff's lawyer. He, a smooth talking, small town, "do-it-all" attorney, approaches the members of the jury, stares at their eyes, points a long finger at my direction and says, "Dr. Zohar was negligent! Because of his carelessness, Mr. Zimmer (he points at the plaintiff) has lost his elbow joint! Because of this doctor's negligence, Mr. Zimmer is not the man he used to be. He can't swim in the river, he can't bow-hunt, he can't use his gun, he can't fish. Because of this negligent doctor, my client can't role on the carpet with his grandkids. And consider the impact of Dr. Zohar's malpractice on Mrs. Zimmer, (he points to the plaintiff's wife). She is the one who has to carry, in deep snow, water to the horses. No more can she enjoy rides with her husband on their Harley Davidson…" The counsel lowers his voice to a hush, "Since mistreated by Dr. Zohar my client and his wife's sex life …". The members of the jury— seven women, four of them could be anyone's grandmothers, and an obese farmer in denim overall—listen attentively but show no visible emotions.

"The defense rests", concludes the plaintiff's counsel. Jessica, my lawyer—a statuesque, blond lady in her early 40's— has already presented her closing arguments. Now the white haired, mustachioed Judge calmly lectures the jury about the methodology of reaching their verdict. I look at the jury and think: Do these old women understand the case? Could they follow the medical evidence presented to them by the experts? Do they possess any commonsense? Are they emotional, favoring the poor fat truck driver—a good old Iowa boy—and his toothless wife, over that rich surgeon (aren't all surgeons rich?) with the foreign accent? Yes, on the paper, we have made our case; we should win—but will we?

Why was I sued? The plaintiff—with a can of beer in his hand—rolled over his lawnmower, sustaining a deep laceration to the region of his left elbow. He was brought to the emergency room of our small rural hospital. The single orthopedic surgeon in town was out of town so I was summoned to treat him. I did not find evidence of vascular or nerve injury; radiography excluded any bony injuries. Three hours after the injury, I took the patient to the operating room and cleansed the heavily contaminated wound. The underlying elbow joint appeared intact so I sutured the laceration and sent him home on antibiotics. I closely followed up the progress of the wound—seeing the patient in office every few days. The wound was swollen but healing with good range of elbow motions. The patient returned to work. Five weeks later, Mr. Zimmer returned with evidence of pus formation deep in the wound. Now I suspected septic arthritis—infection within the joint space. I summoned the orthopedic surgeon, who took over the case. The patient required two additional operations to treat, first the septic arthritis, and a few months later, the adjacent osteomyelitis. He lost some function of the elbow and required long-term antibiotics.

I learned about the lawsuit almost a year after I had left Iowa. On reading the accusations against me, my reaction consisted of anger combined with surprise and frustration. Anger of being sued after providing the best care I could. Anger for the undermining of my self-esteem (e.g. "who are they to tell me how to treat surgical infections? I wrote books about surgical infections…"). Anger and frustration for the hassle, which I knew, would be prolonged. Surprise, because I remembered Mr. Zimmer very well as a "nice guy", with whom I seemed to have formed a friendly rapport.

The allegations against me hinged on the "expert" opinion of an orthopedic surgeon from a leading hospital in Baltimore. At his deposition, the expert claimed that I had deviated from the standard of care by not calling an orthopedic surgeon to treat the laceration, and by not testing the joint to detect injury that was thus missed—resulting in the infection.

A date for the trial had been scheduled but, as commonly is the case, the plaintiffs' side came up with an offer to settle before trial, asking for $ 90,000. The offer was declined. My lawyer and the insurance company decided to battle the case in court.

A month before the trial, I was summoned by my lawyer to attend a "mock trial", conducted by a Chicago-based trial consulting company. We met in a hotel near Minneapolis. My lawyer acted the role of the plaintiff's counsel. The "trial consultant"—a forty something African-American woman—videoed the mock trial. She then re-played the tape to us, critiquing my performance, "Sit straight, keep your head up, do not look defensive, look at the jury, maintain eye contact; take your time, listen to the questions, think—count, silently, to four before speaking—do not let them pace you…" After lunch, we repeated the performance. "Much better! Now you look the sympathetic doctor the jury has to see. We want you to reflect an image of a warm, caring doctor…" My lawyer added, "Remember, your task is to answer the factual questions the best you can—nothing more. Leave the rest—the actual defense of what you did, and how good you think you are, to our expert witnesses and me."

A few months later, on the eve of the trial, we checked into a cozy riverside inn in Fort Madison. The Chicago legal consultant arrived as well. Yet again, I was briefed, questioned and criticized, including the color of my shirt and the tie to go with it.

Day 1 in court: I sit at the side of my lawyer on the defense bench. I try to appear serious and somber. I look directly at the jury and know they are observing my body language. The morning hours are consumed by the selection of the jury. My lawyer memorizes the names of the fifteen-jury candidates in five minutes. For a long hour, she is interviewing them, calling each in his name, without consulting her notes. In the afternoon, both sides present their opening statements. My lawyer is well prepared: She presents the jury with large posters depicting the sequel of events, the main issues to be considered, how she is going to argue for me and who will be our expert witnesses. She ends by telling the jury a little about my professional background. Already the differences in style between both sides are apparent: the plaintiffs' counsels are repetitive and emotional—preaching as if in an Evangelic church; my lawyer—straightforward, accurate, cool, and rational.

Day 2 in court: the plaintiff, followed by his wife, takes the witness stand. They recount all the miseries caused by my alleged mistreatment. My lawyer's cross-examination of them is brief and polite. "We have to appear sympathetic to them," she whispers on my ear, "we don't want to rub the jury the wrong way…"

After lunch, I am climbing onto the witness stand. I have been prepared and tutored *ad nauseum*; I know the records of this case by heart, I know which questions my lawyer will ask me, and I know what I am going to say. Still, I do not remember myself being so anxious for many years. Yes, I know that my life or livelihood does not depend on the outcome of this trial. But my honor and professional self-esteem does, the risk of losing fuels my anxiety. Replying to my lawyer questions about my professional life and the case's events goes smoothly. Even the cross examination seems surprisingly easy. I count to four before replying, I look humbly at the jury, I occasionally slow the plaintiff's counsel pace by asking, "Please could you repeat your question." My lawyer takes over again and asks me a few more questions. "I'm going to clear the shit after you, clarifying anything which you screw up", she promised beforehand.

Day 3 is dedicated to the expert witnesses on both sides. The defense's orthopedic expert from Baltimore is the first to appear—but not in person. It seems that the avid expert is not too keen to travel to remote, frozen rural locations, especially when he has to appear in some court twice a month. Thus, his method is to testify on video, captured in Baltimore, a week prior to the trial. In the first hour of the video, the orthopedic surgeon is questioned by the plaintiffs' lawyers about how I deviated from the standard of care. My lawyer, on her cross-examination, goes straight for his jugular. The jury learns the following: that the expert has never practiced outside an urban academic hospital; that he is a habitual expert witness for plaintiffs against surgeons, deriving 50-60 % of his income from work as an expert witness: that he had testified against doctors around the country including in Delaware, North Carolina, Pennsylvania, Connecticut, Texas, Utah, Florida, Washington, D.C, Missouri, Maryland, Arizona and Minnesota; and that during the last five years he earned "about $ 200,000 or slightly more" per year as an expert witness.

Next, my lawyer calls on the experts for the defense. Two of them are orthopedic surgeons, one of whom the chief of orthopedic trauma in a local University Hospital. The third is a general surgeon in practice. All are in their early fifties, well-groomed and eloquent—good old Iowa boys. They seem to be well pre-rehearsed by my lawyer. They provide an opinion opposite to that of the Baltimore boy—that I practiced within the standard of care. That the various tests to check for joint injury, which were mentioned by the plaintiff's expert, are controversial and not the standard of care. On painstaking cross-examination, the plaintiff's lawyers tries to confuse and discredit our experts with many "hypothetical" questions. However, it seems to me that "my" experts are well received and appreciated by the jury. After all, they represent the home team—not Baltimore.

Day 4 in court. The last day. Closing arguments. As always, the plaintiff's lawyer begins. The same emotional delivery. "Do not be influenced by the number of the experts on the defendant's side", he preaches the jury, "all experts are well paid for their time. Supported by the malpractice insurance company the defendant can afford any number of experts—we can't! What matters are the facts of the case, the evidence! Follow the evidence presented to you—not the number of the defense experts."

Now, Jessica, my lawyer stands up. She summarizes the events of the case. She lectures about the difference between "complications", as opposed to "adverse outcomes", "malpractice" or "negligence. She speaks about the "'Monday morning quarterback", alluding to people who criticize or pass judgment from a position of hindsight. She concludes, "This trial has focused on the unfortunate injury sustained by Mr. Zimmer— and rightly so—on the suffering it caused him and his wife, for whom we are all, including my client, very sorry. But please, do consider that by ruling for Mr. Zimmer not only you will award compensation to the Zimmer family but also you will be unjustly punishing my client. The defense rests your honor."

Such little legal saga of mine is not unique. Thousands of surgeons find themselves in that situation each year—at least one third having committed no error at all. A random sample of 1452 "closed" malpractice claims, from five liability insurers, showed that more than one third of the claims appeared to be frivolous and that the majority of such "unjustified" claims (84 percent) did not result in compensation, while most that involved injuries due to error did. However, this is hardly comforting to the surgeon who has to defend such frivolous claim: the many uncompensated days, the travel expenses, and the cost of strain. This study also showed that for every dollar spent on compensation, 54 cents went to administrative expenses—including those involving lawyers, experts, and courts[1]. Clearly, a large army of legal and paralegal "parasites" is nourished by this system.

In my case, the two small town lawyers knew where to find the famous "orthopedic legal whore"; they could count on him to come up with some pseudo academic list of alleged errors committed. They probably guessed that their chance to win is no more than 50/50 but they did not invest much in this case except a few hours of sporadic work, and the $ 8000 paid to the Baltimore surgeon. So, if the plaintiff's lawyers have nothing to lose—why shouldn't they sue indiscriminately, hoping for an occasional downfall of a million…

This case taught me also that, generally, the litigated physician, nonetheless his distress and hassles, has a significant advantage over the litigating patient. A generously funded expert legal team and the ability to hire an impressive "home team" of experts are hard to bit by a meager suing team. In order to prevail, the plaintiff has to be represented by solid lawyers, his expert witness has to know his job and, above all, the case against the physician has to be bulletproof.

Back to the case of Dr. Conway. As I opened the transcript her deposition, I believed that we had a good case against her. As I browsed through the document, I found nothing to change my mind.

---

[1] 1. Studdert DM, Mello MM, Gawande AA, Gandhi TK, Kachalia A et al. Claims, errors, and compensation payments in medical malpractice litigation. N Engl J Med. 2006;11;354:2024-33

11

The transcript of Dr. Conway's deposition by Veronica Chapman was relatively lightweight at only 56 pages. The deposition took place in the defense lawyer's (Francis Z. Furrer, III) office in Gulfport—the surgeon's hometown.

I cruised rapidly through the preliminary trivia, highlighting only items that caught my eyes as pertinent; or adding some light on the surgeon's personality.

Veronica asks: "Okay. And what specifically brought you to Adventist Medical Center?"

The surgeon replies: "I grew up in New Orleans and wanted to get closer to home and family. So there were a lot of openings for physicians after Hurricane Katrina and the hospital was looking to start a general surgery practice, so I applied and got the position."

"Veronica: "Okay. And your medical specialty is, you're just a general surgeon; is this correct?"

"I'm a general surgeon, not just," replies the surgeon.

Great answer to a misguided remark by a green lawyer, I thought.

Veronica: "I didn't mean to diminish your specialty by any means."

"That's okay," replies the surgeon.

A few pages later, Veronica asks: "And are you married?"
"Yes."
"Okay, and what does your husband do for a living?"
"He is a neurosurgeon."
"And where does he work?"
"At the Adventist."

Ah, so she is married to a big fish, a neurosurgeon. A couple like this, a general surgeon and a brain surgeon, bring lots of money to the hospital. They are invaluable and irreplaceable. The hospital will do anything to defend her. *They would not want to piss her husband.*

At last, on page 10, Veronica arrives at Katrina's case. After hearing from Dr. Conway that she had reviewed the patient's chart and operative notes on the previous day, she asks when was Katrina's umbilical hernia diagnosed.

The surgeon speaks about the lipoma that she had removed previously from the patient's back. "Probably at that time I have noted the hernia, and with that diagnosis, I would have seen her in the office a week prior to surgery, and we went over hernia repair and our plan."

Veronica: "Okay. Tell me about that office visit. You had said you had discussed a hernia repair with her. What would you have discussed?"

The surgeon: "In any patient who is undergoing surgery, I would examine the patient, get their full history and physical, and make a diagnosis and then explain how we're going to repair the hernia. And that would include—in this case, it was a laparoscopic hernia repair."

She does not answer the question, I thought. She talks about "any patient"—not "my" patient. She talks about what she *would* do, not what she did. Because she did not document the encounter with the patient. Is Veronica smart enough to point this out?

Veronica continues: "Okay. Now tell me—I want you to, if you would, doctor, teach me a little bit about a hernia repair. Tell me specifically what was going on with Ms. Katrina Gospel."

Dr. Conway:" So a hernia is a hole in the muscle. And the reason we treat hernia is to prevent intestine or other abdominal contents from getting stuck within the hernia. So that's why it had to be treated. They also cause pain and discomfort but really, the main objective of hernia repair is to prevent incarceration and strangulation of the intestine." *This is what she is telling her patients*, I thought, while the truth is that an umbilical hernia in such an obese patient is very unlikely to have intestine "getting stuck within it" or being strangulated. As to the "pain and discomfort"—did Katrina really complain about it?

As if having read my thoughts, Veronica asks: "Was she in pain? Do you recall her complaining of pain?"

Dr. Conway: "I do not really."

Veronica hands a copy of the operative report to the surgeon: "I want to kind of just walk through this with you. I have some things that I'd like for you to explain to me just kind of step by step."

After the surgeon confirms that this is her own operative report, Veronica questions her about each sentence: the type of anesthesia, the patient position, the preparation and draping of the operative field, the insertion of the Veress needle.

"Doctor," she asks, "in the next sentence you wrote, 'a Veress needle was inserted within the right upper quadrant in the usual fashion. What is the usual fashion?"

Dr. Conway: "So the needle is passed through the abdominal wall, through the subcutaneous tissues, the muscle, the fascia and into the peritoneum."

Veronica: "Okay. It says here 'the insufflation tubing was attached to the Veress needle and the reading on the monitor read occluded'. Right?"

"Uh-huh".

Veronica: "And what does it mean?"

"So after placing the needle in, the insufflation tubing was attached to the needle and the pressure within the abdominal cavity is read on the monitor. And on the monitor—the word 'occluded' came up".

Veronica: "Okay. And later I want to talk a little bit more about the actual machine that you used. So you were getting the reading from where?"

"Off the machine. From a screen, a computer, a computerized screen."

Veronica: "Okay. And it says here that the needle was then removed and placed through the same puncture site again and the monitor read—you had the same reading on the monitor. It says here that you're inspecting the needle. What specifically you were looking for?"

"I was looking if any tissue were stuck in the needle, to make sure it looked like it was functional and not occluded with any debris or tissue or fluid."

Veronica: "Okay. And it says here, 'the tubing was noted to be functional'—"

"Yes. So I asked the nurses to turn the machine on and make sure air was coming out, you know CO_2 was coming out of the tubing."

The next two pages of the deposition are chitchat about whose responsibility is to check the insufflation machine before the operation (the nurses'). Then Veronica asks:

"Doctor, there is a sentence here that, after the third time that you inserted the needle, 'the pressure was noted to increase at 20 almost immediately'. What significance does that have to you?"

"That's a high pressure. So when placing the needle through the abdominal wall, once the needle clicks and is in the proper position, the pressure within the abdomen is lower than 20," replies the surgeon.

"So this reading of 20 is telling you that it's still not the right spot, right?" Veronica asks.

"It's not in the correct spot, correct," Dr. Conway admits.

Veronica: "Okay. And that combined with the sentence in your report which reads, 'the abdomen appears not to insufflate, and then again the monitor read occluded…so those things were other signs to you, correct, that the needle was not in the right place?"

"Yes".

Veronica: "But at this time—this is when it says, according to the operative report that 'the CRNA, Mr. Thorp, noted there was change in the patient's condition', correct? Please tell me doctor what happened in the OR at that time, what was said to you and what you recall?"

Dr. Conway: "She was hypoxic and hypotensive and there was concern—basically the patient was coding. And at that time, in any operation, if the patient's vital signs are changing, you abort the procedure and you figure out what's going on with them."

Veronica: "How much time had passed, if you recall, from the time you had made the first attempt to insert the needle to this point in the procedure?"

Finally, a good question, I thought. The right answer would be not more than five minutes, perhaps less.

"Not very long at all. I don't know," replies the surgeon.

"A minute, two minutes? That's fine if you don't recall," says Veronica.

Why is Veronica so gentle with Conway? Of course, she recalls. Any surgeon would remember such case until the end of her career. But Conway talks about the case as if it happened to another surgeon—so vague and remote.

"I don't know, but not very long at all." *She is stubborn.*

Veronica continues: "And you had mentioned that she started coding; there was change in her vital signs. Where these observations that you made independently or did Mr. Thorp inform you of this? Tell me how that came to be?"

"So in the OR, we all kind of work together. Now, as a surgeon, my focus needs to be on my patients, their operation, so I'm not watching the monitor. So exactly the time, I don't know. But the CRNA alerted me about the coding and we started ACLS protocol, you know, CPR. Which included chest compressions, checking that the endotracheal tube was in the correct position, we ordered chest X ray, all the routines, you know."

Veronica: "And the labs, what specifically are you testing for with the labs?"

Dr. Conway: "So full lab panel being cardiac enzymes, basic chemistries, CBC, ABG."

Veronica walks at the periphery of the issue, I thought. The "correct" questions to ask would have been: what went in your mind when you heard that the patient is coding? What did you think was the reason for the collapse? What was your differential diagnosis?

The plaintiff's lawyer talked to the defendant-doctor as if one would talk to a psychiatric patient in order not to upset her too much.

12

I continued reading Dr. Conway's deposition.

Veronica: "Okay. It says here, I quote, 'her chest X ray was within normal limits'. It says 'a TEE was performed'. Tell me briefly what a TEE is?"

"Trans—it's an echocardiogram. I can't remember what the middle "E" is."

Veronica: "I think the "E" stands for "esophageal", it is transesophageal echocardiogram. OK, let's see, and it says here that 'she was noted to have air within the heart on both the right and left sides'. What is that telling you?"

"So with that there's a concern of where this air came from."

Really. Didn't she know where the air was coming from?!

Veronica: "Is the TEE an immediate test, so the result was immediate—"

"Yes, it's done bedside, so all of this is being performed at the same time—"

At this point Mr. Furrer, the defense attorney, interferes: "You all have to stop talking over each other. Both of you."

Veronica: "Sorry, I'm just getting into the conversation. That's all. I'm trying to understand what happened. I'll let you finish, Doctor."

Dr. Conway: "How about another question."

Amazing, I thought. Finally, Veronica is on the right track. She is talking about the TEE, the test that proved that the cause for the patient's collapse was air emboli. Her next question should concern the timeline—how many minutes from the patient's 'coding' was the result of the TEE available? Instead, the defense attorney injects his admonition and manages to interrupt Veronica's thought process. And even the defendant, rather than kept on the defense, gets more confidant, asking for "another question". Veronica complies—like a good, well-mannered pupil.

Veronica: "Okay. Fair enough. Again, the next sentence says, 'At this time, a Cordis and Swan-Ganz catheter was inserted. Am I pronouncing this correctly?"

"Yes," confirms the surgeon.

"Okay. What is the significance of that? What does it do?"

"That is a type of i.v line. A Cordis is an introduction line. It's a large bore introducer line to obtain i.v access—into a central large vein. You can infuse also fluids. But specifically a Swan-Ganz catheter can be threaded through the Cordis, and that is a catheter that passes through the heart and the tip of it is lodged within one of the pulmonary vessels."

The next question should have been, I thought, about the need for such procedure, which would have been to aspirate air from the chambers of the heart, and again about the time line— how long it took to complete it. But Veronica is moving on.

Veronica: "And it looks like she was placed in a different position at this time, as well?"

"Yes," confirms the surgeon.

"Tell me about the significance of placing her in a different position."

"Once the air was identified within the heart, we positioned her to prevent any air from leaving her heart to go to the other structures."

She should have been more specific. The so-called Durant's maneuver consists of tilting the patient on her left side in order to keep the air bubble in the right side of the heart, preventing it from travelling into the pulmonary arteries and obstruction by "air lock" the blood flow to the left side of the heart. At the same time, placing a patient in the Trendelenburg, head down, position would prevent air embolism from traveling to the brain, causing a stroke. The question was *incomplete* as well. Veronica should have asked about which positon specifically was used. She should have done her homework.

Veronica: "Okay. And can you tell me from your operative report, or from your own recollection, if that repositioning was done immediately, I mean, how much time had passed from when you had aborted the procedure to when you changed her positon?"

"Not long."

"A minute?" asks Veronica.

"I don't know. Not long."

A minute? How naïve to suggest a minute, I thought. Clearly, Conway did not think about air emboli until the TEE had been performed. Surely, the TEE machine, and the cardiologist to perform it, were not sitting there in the OR, awaiting Dr. Conway to produce the air emboli. They had to be summoned. The cardiologist and his machine had to interrupt whatever they were doing at that time and rush to the OR. Ten minutes? Twenty? Who knows? The patient should have been repositioned immediately after she arrested, not many minutes later. As to the insertion of the Cordis and the Swan-Ganz, hard to believe that it was performed earlier than half an hour after the patient's collapse.

However, Veronica does not insist. She changes direction: "Doctor, it says here in your operative report that at some point you elected to assure that the abdomen was completely desufflated of gas and that you made a midline incision into the abdomen; is that correct?"
"Correct."
"Please Doctor, walk me through the procedure."
"OK. Well, because there was air within the heart I wanted to be assured that she didn't have any ongoing bleeding, nor any continued air within the abdomen. So I opened her abdomen to assure that there was no air in there and also to look and make sure that there was no, you know, blood loss or significant bleeding within the abdomen. And there was no sign or air within the abdomen, nor was there any sign of bleeding when I inspected."
Veronica: "What made you think that there might be air in the abdomen aside from…there was air in the heart, but there had been three attempts to position the needle, all of which had failed. So what made you think that you had actually succeeded in getting air into the abdomen?"
Finally, a good follow-up question. Clearly, there was no point in opening the abdomen at that stage. The likelihood of free gas was zero, and anyway, leaving some gas behind is not an issue. In addition, the "need to exclude intra-abdominal bleeding" was BS. The surgeon was confabulating.
Dr. Conway: "Could you repeat that?" *A smart girl,* I thought. She knows how to slow down the interrogation. How to dictate the pace. Buy time.
Veronica: "There were three attempts to properly insert the needle, correct?"
"Correct."
"All of which failed?"
"Correct," repeats the surgeon.

"And so," Veronica persists, "what made you think that you had succeeded in pumping air into the abdomen when all three attempts to place a needle had failed?"

"Because the tubing was attached to the needle and the insufflation was pumping air through the needle."

Veronica: "But you observed there was no air that came out of the abdomen, correct?"

"Correct."

Veronica: "So after this, after you do this procedure, Mrs. Gospel is then taken out of the operating room, and where is she brought?"

Again the lawyer retreats, instead of pushing on—to force the surgeon, step by step, to admit that the indication for opening the abdomen was non-existent.

A few pages down the deposition's transcript Veronica attempts to discuss the insufflation machine—the machine that pumps the CO_2 during laparoscopic surgery.

"This is a copy of the manual of the machine that Francis, I mean Mr. Furrer, provided to us. And I just want to kind of get a better idea of how it works. "

The defense attorney interferes: "Sure, that's fine. I will tell you, you can ask anything, and to the extent she knows how the machine works, she can answer. I don't think she's the person that operates the machine or has all the knowledge, but whatever she knows, it's fair to ask."

Baloney. A laparoscopic surgeon who has no understanding of the basics of the insufflating machine is like a pilot who does not know how his airplane flies. Sure, the nurses switch the machine on and off and replace the empty gas tank. But it is the surgeon's responsibility to "fly it with the patient".

Veronica: "I'm just trying to get a better understanding myself of what you were seeing and what was going on, how the machine operates and works. And so I'm just going to ask you some very basic questions about that. And this is, I guess, the best picture here that I found. Does this look like the machine that you were using that day?"

Dr. Conway: "Yes."

Veronica: "And this is a Stryker, 40 liter high flow insufflator. And had you used a machine like this before?"

"Yes."

"And so when you're getting your readings there're on a screen which looks similar to this, correct?"

"Yes."

Veronica: "And, Doctor, so this is the needle, correct, the Veress needle?"

Again she is retreating, I thought, before sapping out the issue. Here was the occasion to ask about the gas flow used. How much CO_2 Conway managed to pump into the patient's abdomen before she collapsed. A dose of 200-300 cc of air injected into a vein is known to be lethal—how many CC's escaped into this patient's vein before Conway stopped the insufflation? This has to be discussed. But Veronica is now focusing on some diagrams and pictures.

"Is this how the Veress needle would be placed? Does this look like the tubing—is this similar to a setup that you were using that day, I guess, is my question?"

"Yes," answered the surgeon.

Mr. Furrer interrupts again: "So the record is clear, what we're doing is looking at three diagrams—the machine, the Veress needle, connected to the tubing…and asking if what is shown is the way that was set up of the day of the procedure. "

Veronica: "Thanks you, Mr. Furrer. Doctor, so again, so what you're doing is you're attempting to insert the needle and then attaching this tube to the end of the needle? Is that how you were—tell me how you utilize this machine. Just kind of describe to me…Go ahead Francis."

The defense lawyers speaks again: "I'm sorry. I'm just not sure—here's like three questions in there. So can we just get one question at a time?"

With his interruptions, I thought, with Conway's staccato, evading answers, they manage to derail Veronica's strategy—if she had any.

Veronica: "Sure, thank you Francis. Okay. You placed the needle inside of Ms. Gospel, correct?"

"Correct."

"Okay. And the next step that you would use in utilizing the machine is to attach it to the needle; is this correct?"

Dr. Conway: "There's tubing that delivers air out of that machine that is attached to the needle, yes."

Veronica: "Let me go back, doctor, and just ask you: how did you learn how to perform this type if surgery?"

"I went to a general surgery residency."

"And you performed this surgery before?"

"Yes."

"How many times before?"

"At least hundreds."

Veronica: "Okay. Have you ever had any complications?"

What a silly question. Of course, she had complications. Every surgeon has complications. Only those who do not operate do not have complications. The correct question would have been: did you ever experience air emboli during one of those operations?

Dr. Conway replies: "No, not like this. I've never seen this. And I've been part of many—thousands of laparoscopic procedures."

So now it is thousands...

Veronica changes the topic: "Doctor, tell me how you chose the puncture site when you first attempted to insert the needle?"

"So in performing an umbilical hernia repairs, trocars are placed on both sides of the abdomen. And you wouldn't want to go midline because that's where the hernia is. You have to have room to perform the surgery. And in performing laparoscopy, you have to be away from the site of surgery, so that's why I chose that side."

"And, what would be an alternate?"

"Either the right side or the left side."

"Okay. But is there a reason why you would choose the right side over the left side or the left over the right?"

"No. There's nothing anatomic to suggest either one is any better."

"Have you ever heard of the *Palmer Point*?"

"Yes."

"Can you tell me what that is?"

"That's when you place the needle on the left side."

"Which is a different side than where you placed the needle, correct?"

"Correct."

"Is there a reason why you would choose the *Palmer Point* over the point where you inserted the needle?"

"No."

"Is it any safer to use the *Palmer Point*?"

"No"

"What makes you draw that conclusion?"

"Because you're sticking a needle through the abdominal wall, and if you were to put the needle through the abdominal wall and injure something, it wouldn't matter—no matter what, if something is injured it would have to be fixed."

"Okay. Let me ask you this: Was Ms. Gospel—would you consider her an obese woman?"

So again, I thought, the defense lawyer retreats, just when she can score a good point. She should have asked: could you define more precisely the *Palmer Point*—isn't it three cm' below the left costal margin in the midclavicular line? Could you tell us why many surgeons consider it the safest access point, when the midline cannot be used? What abdominal organs and blood vessels are situated in the right upper quadrant as opposed to the left? So what structures could be at risk during the insertion of the needle on the right as opposed to he left? But Veronica accepts the "no's" of the surgeon. There is no attempt to confuse, agitate, fluster. Nothing.

"Yes." Dr. Conway agrees that the patient was obese.

Veronica: "Okay. Does that influence your decision on where to choose the puncture site? Does the weight make a difference?"

"Weight makes a different in any surgery. It makes it more difficult if you're having to pass through four inches versus no inches of abdominal wall. You know, it's a shorter path in somebody who's smaller."

Obviously, I though, Conway enjoys explaining the basic surgical facts to a layperson. Perceptive lawyers know how to exploit that common instinct of the physician to teach—to display his knowledge; they let him speak and speak—waiting for her to reveal more information or to contradict herself. Veronica appears to be a novice. She could ask: and what about the liver in obese patients? Is it laden with fat? Wouldn't a fatty, enlarged liver be more prone to injury by the Veress needle inserted in the right upper quadrant?

Instead, Veronica asks: "Do you think Ms. Gospel's weight was one of the reasons you had difficulty in placing the needle in the proper place?"

"Yes."

Conway is smart. Yes and no. She seems well prepared by her lawyer.

Veronica: "Tell me about what significance the angle of the needle when you're trying to insert it has on whether it's properly placed? Are you just putting it straight through or do you position it at a 45-degree angle, or what angle does it come in at?"

Conway: "So in an obese patient, you're going to go 90 degrees to the abdominal wall. Whereas in a smaller patient, normal BMI, you would insert it at a 45-dgree angle because there's less abdominal wall to pass through."

"Okay. And you had talked about, of course, you were using the machine to confirm the proper needle placement, but are there alternate ways to confirm proper needle placement other than using the machine?"

"Could you say that one more time?" *Good tactic.* She heard the question all right but needs a breather. No "please". A tough woman.

Veronica repeats her question. Conway answers with "yes."

"Okay," says Veronica, "can you describe some of those to me?"

"The saline drop test is a well-described way."

"Tell me about that. Tell me what the saline drop test is."

"So you put saline in the Veress needle. And if it drops into the abdomen, it will help confirm whether or not you're in. But it isn't proven as necessary, nor it's the standard of care. Certainly attaching the insufflation tubing to the Veress needle is a perfectly well-described way of assuring where you are. Besides, the needle has a built-in mechanism where it will click if you're in the right place. And that's what I did that day and everyday that I perform these surgeries."

Veronica: "Had you used the saline drop test before?"

"Yes," admits the surgeon, "but not recently."

Veronica: "Are there other ways of confirming proper placement of the needle besides the machine and the saline drop test?"

"Say that one more time," asks the surgeon. The lawyer repeats the question.

The surgeon replies: "Well. There are other ways, but I'm not an expert in those."

Veronica: "Are you familiar with an aspiration test?"

"Sure. You can aspirate any needle and see if blood comes back."

"Okay. But that wasn't a test you used?"

"No. I do not use this test."

Veronica:"The saline drop test, the aspiration test, are those recognized methods of proper needle placement in the medical community?"

"Say that again." Veronica says it again.

The surgeon replies: "Yes. But also confirming where you are by attaching the insufflation tubing and checking the pressure is also an acceptable way to confirm placement."

Veronica: "How many attempts would you normally make in placing the needle before aborting a procedure?"

"Probably three."

"Is three the standard of care?"

"Never have—never had a chance to go to another site in any patient."

She does not answer the question. But again Veronica withdraws: "Okay. So obviously at some point an air embolism formed, correct, in Ms. Gospel. Tell me what the significance of having air around her heart chamber?"

"The air can leave the heart and go to other parts of the body and damage other organs."

"Including the brain?"

"Yes".

"Okay. And that's what happened with Ms. Gospel, correct?"

"Yes," confirms the surgeon.

Veronica: "One part of the record reflects that blood was aspirated from the ventricle and that there was a copious amount of air within the aspirated blood. What does that indicate to you?"

"That there's air within the heart. The Swan–Ganz catheter was positioned and the port on the catheter was aspirated, and then they got air out."

Rubbish, I thought, there is no data to support emergency catheter placement for air aspiration during an acute setting air emboli causing hemodynamic instability.

Veronica: ""How much air around the heart could be tolerated."

No "around", silly, "inside" the heart.

"I don't know," replies the surgeon.

Veronica moves to the topic of hyperbaric chamber in which the patient was placed in the attempt to improve oxygenation of her injured brain. Dr. Conway admits that the patient arrived at the chamber "approximately two hours from the start of the code."

Waste of time—much too late for hyperbaric chamber to do anything good.

Veronica plods on: "Doctor, after Ms. Gospel was stabilized, did you see her again?"

"Oh yes. I followed her entire hospital stay, her month-and-a-half stay at Adventist. She was on my service and I took care of her."

Not exactly, what the patient had claimed in her deposition.

After a few pages, dealing with the patient's stay in the hospital and questions about changes in her physical and mental status ("I'm not a neurologist", "I'm not a psychiatrist", replies the surgeon) Veronica asks this:

"Did you have discussions with any of your colleagues about what happened?"

"Yes, and everybody's opinion was and is that I did everything correctly."

Veronica: "If you did everything correctly, then why did everything go so bad?"

"I'm going to object to the form of that, Veronica," interjects the defense lawyer.

"Okay, let me rephrase that question. So if everything went correctly, then how did an air embolism form in Ms. Gospel"?

"While it's unfortunate that this happened to her, it's a well described complication that can occur with laparoscopy. It's in every surgery textbook. It's an unfortunate thing that happened. And it's certainly… you know…nothing was done maliciously."

So, *if it's in every textbook why did you not know how to prevent it?* I would have asked this question.

Veronica: "Isn't it true that it's a rare complication?"

"Yes. Extremely rare. 0.001 %."

"And in your opinion, what happened?"

"What do you mean by that?"

"How did the air embolism form, in your opinion?"

"Aha. Air must have gotten out of that machine and into her body though the needle."

"Through an improper placement, right?"

"Object to the form. You can answer," says Mr. Furrer.

Dr. Conway: "The needle is passed blindly through the abdominal wall. You cannot see every vein. You cannot prevent a vein from being punctured. Certainly, there was no sign that I was in a vein. There was no blood coming out of that needle."

Bullshit, I thought. You could prevent or diminish the chances of venous punctures by inserting the needle in the left site. You could know that you are in the vein by aspirating on the needle—there was no blood coming out of that needle because you did not aspirate it.

"And it's an unfortunate thing that happened to her, and we did everything we could to take care of her," adds the surgeon.

Veronica: "If you had used any of the additional tests that we talked about—"

"It wouldn't have made a difference." Conway does not wait for the lawyer to finish her question.

"Doctor, on what sort of literature do you rely on to support your opinion that it wouldn't have made a difference? Do you rely on any literature?"

"Yes."

"Okay. What pieces of literature?"

Now Mr. Furrer comes to the aid of the surgeon: "If you don't know off the top of your head, I mean, we can certainly provide that information later."

The surgeon grabs the rescue ring: "Okay. I don't know off the top of my head, but I do have a paper that supports what I did. And my experience also supports what I did and what I do every day."

She really believes that what she did was perfect.

After a quick break, the deposition resumes. Veronica decides to re-examine a few topics:

"Doctor, going back to your reposition of Ms. Gospel after you have aborted the position, tell me specifically in what position you laid her in?"

"The left lateral decubitus position—the left side is placed down and the right side up."

"And the significance of this position is…I think you touched it briefly earlier."

"So that prevents air—it creates an air lock to keep the air within the heart chamber so that it cannot go through the valves and to the rest of the body."

Veronica: "Okay. But at that point, in your opinion, the air…had it already gone to other parts of Ms. Gospel's body?"

"Yes."

"So does that positioning relieve any air or un trap any air?

"No."

"So how do you remove the air once it's inside the body?"

"It's absorbed through…the body absorbs it. And this is the theory behind the hyperbaric chambers, absorbs that air."

"Okay," Veronica continues," How long was Ms. Gospel in that left-sided position? How long did you leave her in that position?"

"She was in the OR over a two-hour period. I would say—I don't know specifically, but—I just don't know—I don't know, but she was in the OR for two hours, so it was during that time."

Here, I thought, the surgeon seems getting confused and emotional. This would have been an opportunity to have her admit that the patient was placed in that position too late.

Veronica: "I want to read to you the previous written answer to our preliminary Interrogatory Number 5. It said: 'Dr. Conway did not perform a saline drop test or other test to be sure the needle was not within a solid organ or a blood vessel because if the pressure in high on the monitor or if the monitor reads occluded, you almost immediately know that the needle is not in the right place.' Doctor, almost immediately—is it an instant response?"

Conway: "It's quick. It's very quick."

How quick? She should have asked the surgeon, how quick—how many seconds would pass until the monitor reports 'occluded'? And meanwhile? What happens meanwhile—how many cc' of gas can be pumped into the patient's vein?

Last few pages of the transcript. Unsurprisingly Dr. Conway again denies any deviation from the standard of care. I found her final replies fascinating.

Veronica: "Is it true that the patient developed an air embolism?"

"Yes."

Veronica: "And isn't it true that you caused that air embolism in Ms. Gospel?"

"No."

Veronica: "Then what caused it?"

Defense lawyer: "If you know. You can't answer if you don't know."

Conway: "I don't know. I don't know."

Veronica: "But in your opinion, it wasn't from any action that you took? You did not cause the air embolism, doctor?"

"No."

"Who did?"

"It's a complication of the surgery."

"So the surgery itself caused it?"

"Yes."

"And you were in charge of the surgery?"

"I performed the surgery."

"And isn't it true that the air embolism caused Ms. Gospel's brain injury?"

"Yes."

Veronica: "No further questions."

End of the transcript.

So no, it was not her—the surgeon—to be blamed for the air emboli. Why should she be blamed? You have to blame *surgery*. Perhaps one could sue *surgery* itself. Let us just see, I thought, how the jury will react when confronted with such bizarre statements. After all, anything said by the witness during the deposition may be used at trial to impeach the witness's' trial testimony—if the latter is inconsistent with what was said during the deposition.

In my mind, Dr. Conway did rather well at her deposition. She had a tough case to defend but she acted according to the usual strategies recommended to defendant physicians: be cool, polite, professional, and brief; offer as much information as necessary—nothing more. Say "I do not know", do not admit any error, do not let them rush you. In brief—show them that you are a robust opponent that they would not be able to plough through in court. That guy Furrer did a great job preparing her.

On the other hand, I was not too impressed with Veronica. Her inexperience was screaming off the pages. She repeatedly committed a crucial sin: "Don't let the witness get away with giving you a vague answer. Force her to be specific!" She asked too many open ended questions that allowed the defendant to say whatever she wished. She should have used many more leading questions—questions that call for "yes" or "no", suggest the answer, or even contain within it the answer.

She should have asked: "Dr. Conway, is it true that during the operation you have injected air into the vein of this patient, which caused air embolism and damaged the patient's brain?" Whatever the surgeon's answer— "yes" or "no" —it could be used against her. Another question that I would ask at the end of the deposition: "Doctor, would you do something differently if you were doing this case today?" A "no" answer could suggest a callous doctor who does not learn from a bitter experience; a "yes" answer hints to the admission of error and culpability.

She should have consulted me before deposing the surgeon. I could have helped her to formulate ensnaring questions. I also did not understand where was her senior partner, Dwight Browning? Why did he let her do it alone when only seventy miles separated his office in New Orleans to the site of deposition in Gulfport.

Conway—what a tough bitch. A hard nut to crack. But towards the end she started showing a few cracks. Unfortunately, Veronica was meandering from topic to topic without managing to hook the surgeon—so that she would not be able to unhook herself during the trial.

Nonetheless, I was optimistic. How can anyone defend this case? My deposition would provide the final knock out!

13

We are seating at the Court Reporter Office in Eau Claire. The defense attorney, Mr. Francis Z. Furrer, II, has just arrived. He is busy unloading a heavy black overnight bag. He arranges files, charts, and a bunch of photocopied papers on the table. He gives us a small node, a tiny smile, and says, "Sorry, I'm a little late."

At the same time, the court reporter organizes her paraphernalia—she will sit on my left side. The video photographer assembles his camera on a high tripod just opposite me—on the other end of the huge oval meeting table. *Don't look at him, just ignore the camera*, I remind myself.

Now, when all his documents are neatly arranged in a few small stacks, Mr. Furrer takes off his gray suit jacket and hangs it on the chair. He stands up and walks around the table to greet us. "Hi Veronica", a pleasant smile—they must have met before in Gulfport. He shakes my hand vigorously, "nice to see you, doctor." He is plumb and short—not taller than I am but seems a few years younger. He turns around and returns to his seat, picks up a yellow legal pad that, I can see, is densely hand written. *Not an iPad lawyer*. He smiles softly at the court reporter and the video guy and shifts his gaze on Veronica: "Are we ready? Everyone ready? I have a flight to catch early afternoon."

"Me too," says Veronica. "We may want to share a taxi."

I begin to like the defense lawyer. I think that this short, chubby and smiley guy in a shabby suit, with his silver hairs, and silver rimmed eyeglasses, could play the role of Mr. Smiley in a movie based on a John Le Carre's novel. Alternatively, with his gentle Southern drawl, Mr. Furrer could have embodied a character directly from one of John Grisham's legal thrillers—one of those righteous, altruistic scholars of law who defend the trodden and poor.

Enough of fiction. This is a nonfiction world and I know very well who Mr. Furrer is. He is a bright and accomplished litigator who has been hired by the Adventist Hospital at Gulfport to exonerate their surgeon. I am sure that he—who during his long career must have sat through many thousands of depositions—has come today well prepared. I am convinced that he has researched my past as deeply as he could; that he can predict what I will say; that his aim today is to unearth the soft spots in me—the spots that he could then lethally penetrate in court. That is, if this case ever reaches the court.

I am prepared as well. Of course, my legal experience is negligible; the number of depositions I sat on is not more than ten. But I am ready for the fight: I know the details of the case by heart, I read vastly around all the pertinent issues; I believe that my "surgical judgment" allows me to define what's wrong and what's right—what is the standard of care. I am confident in my opinions. I know the role of the expert witness. I have even read the book *How to become a dangerous expert witness*—sort of a military manual: know you enemy, learn to control him, win!

However, I am well aware that to a great degree, any malpractice case is a battle between experts. Today is my turn. Tomorrow, the defense will find their own expert—somebody who could convincingly refute my opinion. My task today is to be so convincing so that no respectable surgeon would want to oppose my opinion.

It is 8:30 am. I take a long sip from dregs of the lukewarm coffee in my thermos. I look at Mr. Furrer and give him a small smile—more a grimace. Bring it on. I am ready.

The transcript of my deposition is 171 pages long—three times longer than the defendant surgeon's deposition. Reading the transcript of your own deposition is like watching yourself in a movie. It is amazing how much a person can say during four and a half hours.   And how much of what you say is rapidly forgotten—*did I really say it?* You notice what you should not have said, what you should have said more clearly. You wish you could have been asked the same question again—now your answer would be more biting. But you had your chance. What is done is done—looking at you from the book length document. From which I will cite here only the highlights.

The defense attorney starts with the usual general background questions: my current employment and type of practice—the spectrum and number of procedures I do; the type of patients I refer to tertiary care centers. He dwells on the size of my town and the catchment area of my hospital, inquires names of co-workers and administrators and details about my income.

Then, as expected, he asks, "Doctor, how long have you been in Wisconsin?"

"Now it's almost 11 years."

"You're not from Wisconsin originally?"

"Oh' no. I had a long, long journey coming to Wisconsin."

"Can you give me the summary version of that journey? I'll probably ask you some other specific questions along the way."

I give him a well-rehearsed synopsis of my professional life. I am assuming that Mr. Furrer is well familiar with a more detailed version of my life story. I bet he had ploughed the internet and bookstores for anything I have written, including chats on surgical online discussion forums. Very soon, I am proven right: when I mention that I have left Iowa because of differences with my partner the lawyer offers:

"Dr. Cappucino?"

"No. That was a fictional name I used." I give him the real name of my previous partner.

"Okay," says Furrer.

"Okay what?"

"All right. Well, that answers some questions I have for later."

"Yeah". I can predict what he will ask later but...let him.

Out of the blue, Furrer is talking about money: "Doctor, before I forget, you had sent a request that we send you a check for this deposition before we got here. We got the request, sent it to the people who administer such things, and we were told that a check had been issued. Did you get any check?"

"Yeah. I got the check."

"Okay. Well, I brought a check with me—just in case you didn't get the one by mail...".

"Sure."

"But I'm glad you got the check."

"Yeah. Thank you."

What is his spiel? As usual, the defense is paying for the opposition expert's deposition. He is compensated for his time. So am I. Why talk so much about it?

Mr. Furrer moves on: "Doctor, you're married?"

"Yeah".

"And have three boys?"

"Yes."

"One of then, Sam, Samuel, is a painter?"

"Yeah."

"An artist?"

"Artist, yeah." *So now he wants to demonstrate that he knows everything about me.*

"And I forgot what the other two sons are doing?"

"Gideon is an actor. David's a hotel manager in New York."

"Okay. All very successful it sounds like."

"Well, hopefully."

"They're doing what they like to do?"

"Yes."

"And you've taught them that I would imagine."

"Yes."

A charming Southern gentleman. He will first exhaust you with amiable chitchat and then…I am bracing myself for a protracted session. Impetuous by nature I have to remind myself not to show any signs of impatience.

I take off my wristwatch and place it on the table so I could peak at it without drawing attention. Only ten minutes have passed. Meanwhile Mr. Furrer rumbles on:

"You told me already that part of your goal in your practice is to aim for not having any complications"

"It should be every surgeon's goal."

"All right. But in particular, it would be your goal in a small town because a small-town setting in rural America is much different than what your practice was before that, is that correct?"

"Yes."

"So you're probably more cognizant of that awareness of trying to avoid complications than you might have been when you practiced in New York?"

"Yes. You are right. The common perception is that deaths or complications after operations in a rural hospital are because of the 'inexperienced surgeon or poor care', whereas if the patient dies in the Ivory Tower then he dies 'despite the best efforts of the excellent doctors in a great hospital'—sort of an act of God."

"And you've written about that. Wasn't there a chapter dedicated to rural surgery in your book on surgical complications?"

"Yes. " *Holly shit*. The guy has read everything I have ever written. Now he is busy flattering me. Soon, in an hour or two, he will dig out the shit —out of context shit of course.

"All right. Now, in the surgeries that you perform, do you do laparoscopic procedures?"

"Yes." *Now he starts to come to the point.* He will try to question my expertise in the type of operation performed by the defendant surgeon.

"Very well. So tell me, in your course of training where did you first get training in laparoscopic surgical techniques?"

"This was just before I left South Africa. 1989. The practice of laparoscopy started to be popular during those years. It is then when we began doing laparoscopic cholecystectomies. And then, I continued doing it in Haifa, where we did also laparoscopic operations for hyperhidrosis, which is excessive sweating of the hands."

"In Haifa, Israel, eh? I've never been, but it's supposed to be a beautiful city."

"Yeah. It's on the mountain. A port town. Nice beaches."

He is dancing round you like an agile boxer. I have no choice but to dance along.

"Now you did some training in England, correct?"

"Yes, in Leeds. Mainly colorectal surgery."

"How long where you there?"

"Six months. It was in 1987."

"Not very long?"

"Enough for what I wanted to learn."

"And how was it that you went to England? Was that just a fellowship that you applied for?"

"No. I got it as a prize. They chose me as the best candidate in the surgical board examinations. They sent me there. Fully paid."

"And then after you finished with that you went back to South Africa?

"Yeah."

"And then after South Africa to Haifa?"

"Yes."

"And then from Haifa is when you came to the USA?"

"Yep."

"Tell me about that. What was your reasoning for wanting to leave Israel and come to the United States?"

How predictable. They always ask the same questions, wanting to paint you as some medical fugitive. At least a quarter of doctors practicing in the USA are foreign medical graduates—indeed in some rural and underserved regions the so called "international graduates" are the only doctors available—but here he's hoping to stain my credibility based on my origin. However, I am used to such questions and know to be chatty and brief at the same time:

"Well, one is young, you know. One is ambitious. And the grass seems greener in the other place."

"And how was that experience" asks Mr. Furrer.

"It's difficult. When you are 40-something years old, actually 45, and you were a big shot in one place and you move to a new place, a different language, a different system…it's not easy. You have to adjust."

Mr. Furrer now examines, point by point, very meticulously, my ten years New York City period: hospitals, academic positions, type of operations, teaching of residents, teaching of students. He is not too happy with my brief replies and digs for details. I am not sure what he is trying to achieve—to exhaust me?

At some point, however, following the rule of going around and around, he returns to laparoscopic surgery.

"All right," Furrer says, "earlier I was asking you about your fist training in laparoscopic surgery. You told me about South Africa and Israel. And next you moved to the USA. So tell me: when you were in New York did you receive any specific training in laparoscopic procedures?"

"Look, I was and I'm doing laparoscopic procedures all the time. I'm a qualified general surgeon. I don't need training."

"So you've never received formal training in laparoscopy."

"I don't understand what you mean by formal. In those early days of laparoscopy we learned from colleagues, who learned from experts; we learned from each other, we learned by ourselves. Formal laparoscopic fellowships were established only years later."

"Okay doctor. And what about laparoscopic hernia repairs? Where did you learn to do those?"

I tell him that I went to a few brief courses to see whether I want to do such procedures, that I have did a few in my practice, that I do not see an advantage for those procedures, and therefore I still prefer open surgery for abdominal wall hernias. For in my hands they carry good results. Furrer continues with repetitive questions about which laparoscopic procedures I do. I answer, also repetitively: "cholecystectomies, appendectomies, tubal ligations, ectopic pregnancies…"

Furrer: "All right. Doctor, I'm going to move around a little bit. We'll come back to some of the more specifics of these procedures. You know how this is done. We all have a different road map we're going to follow."

"Sure," I reply. *I know your road map is to tire me out.*

"Tell me about your work as an expert witness. How much work do you do currently?"

This is another obligatory question so I am ready for it as well. I tell him about the sporadic cases I was involved with— "yes, usually on the plaintiff side". Furrer begs for details: where, which State, who was the lawyer—but I offer none. "I don't recall," I answer repeatedly. I know he tries to portray me as a legal whore for the plaintiffs—which I am not.

Suddenly Furrer comes with this: "Did Veronica tell you that this case is set for trial in December this year?"

"Will there be a trial?"

"Well doctor, the date for the trial is set."

"If you invite me, I'll come."

"Well, I think it would be up to them," he points at Veronica, "as to whether they're going to invite you or not."

"I hope the venue for the trial will be nice," I say. I engage mechanically in this chitchat. I believe, however, that there will be no trial. *How would they not settle such case?*

Veronica: "You will receive an invitation, I assure you."

Furrer: "As to the venue, I can promise you one thing: it will be much warmer than it will be here in December."

Furrer starts questioning my relationships with the plaintiff's lawyers and how did I form my opinion about this case. I tell him about getting the opinion of members of an online surgical club: "I presented to them exactly what happened in the OR. I asked them 'what do you think guys?'

Furrer: "And you have all their replies. Could I have copies?"

"Yes. But I will have to delete or hide the names of responders."

"Did you have an opinion before you posted this to the group of what your own thoughts were?"

"Obviously. I think I'm an expert in this field. Otherwise I wouldn't be sitting here, having such a pleasant talk with you."

"And what was your opinion?"

"I found multiple errors in the management of this patient. A chain of errors." I note an angry tone in my voice, I try to suppress it.

"All right. We'll go into those."

"And then you got responses back from various people I would assume in various countries?"

"Yes."

"Can you—do you remember any of those specific responses?"

I tell him.

"Has there been ongoing discussion in recent months about this case?"

"Yes, recently in preparation for this deposition, I wanted to refresh my mind. I ask them again about how they use the Veress needle because I don't use it anymore."

"So why don't you use the Veress needle now?"

"Because , like many other surgeons, I believe that open access is safer."

"And did you use a Veress needle at some point of your career?"

"I used it in the beginning until I was getting fed up with it," I reply.

Asked to be more specific I add, "I used it in South Africa, in Israel, also in the USA, at the beginning, in the early years until about 1998, I think,"

Furrer: "And was there something specific that happened or a scientific article or conference you attended that convinced you that you shouldn't use the Veress needle anymore?"

"No. You know, in surgery there is always a spectrum of options. We try to figure out the option that better suits our patients—that is optimal in our hands. Of course, we are influenced by what we read, what we hear in the meetings, and what our friends are doing, around the world and in our own environment."

"So, if you are not using the needle, how do you gain access for the laparoscopic procedures you are doing?"

I squint at my watch. It is already 10:30. And he's still hovering at the margins of the case. I have to be patient. I reply, as one would talk to a medical student: "Well, I do a small cut in the skin. I expose the fascia. I cut the fascia. I find the peritoneum, lift it up, make a cut in the peritoneum, and check whether I'm inside by putting my finger into the hole, ensuring that it's all free from adhesions and bowel and only then I insert the trocar, a special trocar, we use the Hasson trocar, and connect it to the tubing, and start insufflating the gas."

"Doctor, you keep looking at the stack of papers over on your left when I've asked these few questions. Is there something there that's helping you answer those questions?"

"No, no. Just a stack of a few transcripts of depositions Veronica sent me."

Furrer: "Could I take a look at what you have there?"

"Sure. Be my guest," I answer indifferently.

Furrer: "And maybe this would be a good time to take a break. We've been going for an hour and 35 minutes."

14

I stand up, yawn, and stretch my limbs. I find the toilets and empty my bladder. My coffee thermos is empty. There is no coffee machine at sight. I find a vending machine in the corridor and get a bottle of sparkling water. Here I meet Veronica who is emerging from the "ladies". I note that she has refreshed her lipstick. She smiles: "You're doing well doctor. I see that you're getting a little restless. Try to relax. This may go for a few more hours. Mr. Furrer is a thorough attorney. Very, very smart."

I return to my place and sit down with a deep sigh. The court reporter smiles at me, the video man is getting ready for the next act. Mr. Furrer is still immersed in his folders, chomping on some candy bar. I grab a banana from my backpack and munch it slowly.

Videographer: "We are back on the record."

Furrer: "You said earlier when we were talking about how you might perform certain procedures, that you don't believe that your way is the only way on multiple kinds of surgeries?

"Of course, of course not."

"And there are other options available, right?"

"Yes. There are many options."

"You don't believe it was any breach of the standard of care to perform this surgery laparoscopically, do you?"

"No. Not if the operation would have been indicated." I know that he wants me to answer "yes" or "no" to his leading questions. Thus, I add a "qualifier"

"Do you believe that the operation was not indicated"?

"I don't know because I don't have the material to be able to judge."

""But you have reviewed the pertinent records, right?"

"Sure, but I didn't find any documentation of the preoperative encounter between the surgeon and the patient. Actually, I asked Veronica about this...."

Veronica joins in: "I didn't see any record of that in the records that we have been provided by the hospital."

Furrer: "All right. There's going to be an effort to provide that to you. But what kind of things would you look at to determine whether you think the surgery was indicated or not?"

"Okay. Not all hernias should be fixed. Hernias which are not symptomatic, that do not cause any pain or discomfort or interfere with the quality of life mustn't be fix. So the decision belongs to the patient. He or she must understand the risk-benefit ratio of the repair. So if I had an obese patient like this one, with a small hernia or even a large one, which doesn't cause any problems, I would suggest to her the option of avoiding an operation."

After spending about half an hour on my own malpractice history, insisting on details—lawyers, dates—which I do not provide ("I don't remember")—the defense lawyer returns to the case under discussion.

"Doctor, a few moments ago when I was asking you what you had posted on that surgical discussion forum, and you were saying that the surgeon, Dr. Conway….but—yes, sir, go ahead."

"I didn't mention the surgeon name to anyone."

"I understand, but for our purpose here today, we are talking about Dr. Katlyn Conway, who is a surgeon in Gulfport, Mississippi, and who's, I'm, assuming, a doctor you've never met, correct?"

"Sure."

"If you met her, you didn't know you met her?"

"I did not meet her."

"All right. You may have attended similar conferences with the hundreds or thousands of other surgeons, but you don't remember meeting her, correct?"

"Correct." What a *nudnik*! He gives me a headache.

"All right. So you were saying that Dr. Conway inserted the Veress needle in the right upper quadrant, which you claim is the wrong location?"

"Yes. Correct."

"Why do you say that's the wrong location?"

"Because it's more risky than the other locations. The least risky location would be in the Palmer point at the left upper quadrant. Why choose the more risky site if you can do it in the less risky site?"

"And you have done any research on this particular question?"

"Well, I never heard about anyone using the right upper quadrant. And looking at the literature, it is clear that the Palmer point is the preferred site for the needle insertion. Again: I've never heard or seen anybody using the right upper quadrant."

"You just never heard of it, right?"

"This is what I said."

"Have you ever seen it demonstrated?"

"No."

"Do you go to the American College of Surgeons meeting every year?"

"Sure. Every year."

"And you've never seen it demonstrated there on video in any sense?"

"Not in the right upper quadrant. Unless there are no other options, say there is a huge bellybutton hernia and the left upper quadrant is scarred from previous operations."

"Can you point me to specific research materials that support that opinion?"

"This is the general knowledge, reflected in numerus books and publications. Common knowledge, you know."

"So you believe that not using the left upper quadrant, but instead using the right upper quadrant by itself is a breach of the standard of care of this surgeon, is that right?"

"In this case, yes."

"Why in this case?"

"Because as I told you before," I try hard to sound patient with this legal *nudnik,* "there are other circumstances, like a scarred left upper quadrant..."

"And when you mentioned earlier about the right upper quadrant being more risky than the left, tell me what those risks are that you associate with the right upper quadrant?"

"There are more organs and structures in the right upper quadrant which could be damaged by the Veress needle. The liver, for example, it lies quite low, especially in obese patients. It can be fatty and big, and it's just under the abdominal wall, so the needle can go into the liver and breach a vein. Then there is the inferior vena cava, the portal vein, large veins which can be entered by the needle...."

Furrer: "Those structures could be injured?"

"Yeah, This is what I'm saying...this what happened in this case..."

"I'm just trying to make sure that I understand you doctor."

"Sure, sure. On the other hand, in the left upper quadrant there's only the stomach, which is decompressed, emptied with the NG tube, and thus is not entered by the needle. So this is why entry on the left is safer."

"Is there the possibility of injuring the colon by using the left upper quadrant?"

"In surgery everything is theoretically possible, but injury to the colon from the Veress needle is very very rare. And anyway, you have the colon also on the right. But, may I…may I add something?"

Yes, sir."

"Air emboli were never reported with insertion of Veress needle in the left upper quadrant. It was never reported in open assess for pneumoperitoneum. All published cases that I found of venous embolism to the heart occurred following insertion for the needle in the right upper quadrant."

"And do you have that research?"

"I found a few case reports. The authors admitted mistake. The people who placed the needle in the right upper quadrant and reported air emboli admitted that they were wrong to use the right side. Now, we have to understand that published case reports of complications can be viewed as the tip of the iceberg. For any rare complication published, there are many more left unreported. You know, people do not boast about their complications…"

"All right. Are those articles, just studies of a single event?

"I told you so. Case reports…"

"So it's not a study of any kind of statistically significant number of injuries?"

"Again, there were case reports, case reports. No series". I sense my irritation is mounting. *Cool down.*

"Because it is a rare complication, isn't it?"

"Yes, rare, but again: 9 in 10 such complications are never published or discussed."

"And where do you get that number? Is that your own assumption?"

"Well, we published a book about surgical complications, we have been dealing with this topic all our professional lives, and we know that most complications are swept under the carpet. I mean, people don't go and boast our bad news."

I look at my watch. Is he going to stop for lunch? I am getting tired and hungry but Furrer seems fresh and unfazed. He continues calmly, as if he has the remaining of the day in his disposition.

"Right, well. I understand your belief that most complications aren't published. What I was asking is where you got the 1 in 10 number? Any statistical basis for it, or is it just anecdotal?"

"Maybe anecdotal. There are no figures. And I believe that in real life the ratio could be even higher."

"OK. Well, despite that, you would agree that the injury we are talking about is a very rare occasion."

"Yes, rare, rare. How many times you want me to repeat that this is rare? Rare but shouldn't happen. It's a complication which should not happen if the surgeon does things correctly."

"OK. But let me just make sure we are on the same page. You do agree, based upon what's published, that this injury is a very rare occurrence? Yes?"

"Yes, rare, yeah, rare…". Now I am bored and exhausted at the same time. I could fall asleep.

"And your belief that it may occur more frequently than may be reported in the literature is based upon your own experience and anecdotal information, is that right?"

"Look, it's a common knowledge. All surgeons know it, that we do not ran and advertise our complications. It's the realty of life. There's no point to ask whether it is anecdotal or not. It's a fact. Fact." *Gee, what a jerk!*

"All right. So it's a fact based upon your experience, right?"

"It is a fact of life."

"Well, you don't know—here is my point. You can't know what happens with every doctor in every hospital throughout the United States, can you?"

"No, I don't know about every doctor in the USA," now I'm forcing myself not to scream at him, "but because I worked in many countries and many hospitals, and I was on the editorial boards of a few major surgical journals, I know what things are published. I know how the clinical and academic surgical world functions and thinks. So…"

Furrer changes direction again. He does not move forwards but zig zags: "So, you no longer use the Veress needle, is that right?"

"Didn't I tell you so?"

"And so that would be the early 90's when you used last time the Veress, right?"

"Yes. But nothing has changed in the structure of the needle since. Same needle, same technique."

"Okay doctor, you mentioned earlier that there are ways to determine the proper placement of the needle, even if you're using the right upper quadrant. But I'm a little confused by the various tests and I'm going to need some education?"

Now we go on and on, back and forth, discussing the various tests. Furrer is never entirely satisfied with any of my explanations and insists on clarifications.

"All right, doctor. I think I understand this test. But I just want to make sure I understand it."

"Yeah." *Whatever,* I think, go on repeating yourself.

And he does: "So you put the saline in the syringe, you insert the syringe into the needle and inject the saline. And the first thing is, if it's in the right place, it disappears, I mean the saline."

"Yeah".

"Then you pull back on the syringe and see what you recover, right? If it's nothing, then you feel you're in the right place?"

"Yes."

"Because the saline has gone into the empty space there in the peritoneum?"

"Yes."

"Now if you pull in blood, then you are concerned?"

"Of course."

"Okay. And what would—your concern would be that you're in?

"That you are in a blood vessel, or maybe in the liver."

"All right. "If you are in a blood vessel, would the contents of that blood vessel be under pressure?"

"Well, no if it's in the vein, for the venous pressures are low. But if it's in the artery, a big artery, and accidental arterial entry has been described, blood will come out under pressure. It will be red, pulsatile."

"Pulsating?"

"Pulsatile we call it."

"Pulsatile. Okay. I'm sorry. I'm doing my best. I'm just a lawyer."

"I know." I perceive he is playing the fake modesty game with me. But still, I want to be kind.

"So what kind of pressure we are talking about and how is that measured?"

"Well, measured in millimeter of Mercury, and the venous pressure varies with the cycle of ventilation. During anesthesia, the patient is ventilated—with inspiration the diaphragm goes down and the venous pressure goes up. I would say the average venous pressure would be between 15 to 20 millimeter Mercury."

"And what would the pressure be in an artery?

"Your blood pressure. 120 something. 140."

"I'm hoping that mine's at 120."

"Hopefully, yeah." *Funny.*

It is almost lunchtime. But Furrer's interest in the various tests used to confirm position of the Veress needle is strong as ever:

"Let us revisit the saline drop test. How is that different than the saline injection and aspiration that you mentioned a moment ago?"

"Look, not everyone employs all tests in each and every case. Some would start with the saline drop—they will top up the hub of the Veress needle with saline. Now when they lift up the abdominal wall at the site of insertion they would watch the drop of saline in the hub. If the drop falls down, disappears, they know it is going into a space, the peritoneal space. But if the tip of the needle is sitting at a high pressure zone, like a vein or artery or the liver, the drop won't fall. And again, not everyone would use all tests. People are using their judgement and discrimination based on the specific situation. The site of insertion, number of attempts…"

"All right. So you're not saying that all these tests should have been done the first time, but you're saying these were options?" Now he is trying to have me define those tests as "options".

"Yeah. I would do one of them at least. I would do one of those tests at my first attempt of insertion. Because you're in the right upper quadrant—which you shouldn't have used from the beginning."

"I understand. And if you are—if you were in a vein, would the saline drop?"

"No. It won't!" *Didn't I explain it just a few seconds ago?* "Because the pressure in the vein is higher. The drop won't drop. And maybe venous blood would pour out of the needle, who knows?"

Furrer shifts to a new topic without the briefest pause:

"Dr. Conway does the first insertion, she hooks up the CO_2, the monitor reads occluded?"

"Yes? Is this a question?"

"I just want to play back with you the operation. So she knows she is not moving forward. She starts over?"

"Yes, yes. You know, it takes six seconds until the monitor reports occluded. Six seconds."

"How do you know that?"

"I tested it."

"When did you test it?"

"Last week."

"And the monitor that you have, is it the same?"

"Oh yeah."

"And the monitor that you have is it the same?" he asks the same question again.

"'Yeah." *I managed to surprise him.* He is not ready for this. I feel revived.

"The same model"?

"The same monitor means the same model. The same that appears on the picture of the monitor attached to Dr. Conway's deposition."

"And where did you test it?"

"In the operating room. Before starting a cholecystectomy, before connecting the gas tube to the patient, I told the circulating nurse to occlude the tube, and I watched the monitor."

"And this was done at the County Hospital, where you perform surgery?"

"Yeah."

"Did you have any record of that? Did you write times or the seconds or anything?"

"Of course not. Those monitors do not leave electronic or paper trail of data. I counted the seconds…and by the way, the manual which comes with the insufflating machine states the same."

"And does it say six seconds."

"Yes."

"And what you found was to be true?" Now he is just asking silly questions while his brain tries to assimilate the surprising information.

"True? Sure. You know six seconds is quite long. Listen: One—two—three—four—five—six. Just imagine how much gas could go into the patient in six seconds."

"Did you photograph this testing that you had done?"

"Of course not." *Is he fucking crazy?*

"Did you videotape it? Video it on a phone?"

"I'm not a lawyer."

"All right. Just the answer is yes or no." I see he is irritated.

"No. But you are welcomed to do your own test and video record it…"

Furrer takes a deep breath, shuffles his papers, trying to compose himself.

"All right. So Dr. Conway…".

I interrupt him midsentence: "One more thing. It is not recorded in the op notes but let's assume that…most probably that the insufflator was set at maximal gas flow. This is what most surgeons use. In that setting, the Veress needle, with its limited diameter, cannot deliver more than 3 liter of gas per minute. Now 3 liters per minute means 50 cc per second. It means 300 cc per six seconds. Such volume injected into the vein can be fatal."

Furrer listens patiently, lets me conclude the sentence, waits a few seconds and starts again: "So Dr. Conway removes the needle and then tries again."

"Yes."

"Still in the right upper abdomen?"

"Yes, still the same. Same hole in the skin."

"And is…obviously, you still have a problem with her using the right upper quadrant?"

"Each time, each attempt, I have more and more problems. I'm now full of problems." I feel like I am riding over him. Energized, I allow myself a little sarcasm.

"Do you…is it also a problem that she used the same hole in the skin?"

"It's a problem that she used the right upper quadrant."

"I understand that. You said that."

"No, the skin is OK with me. If she stayed there, in the right upper quadrant, what point would be to make one more hole in the skin? If the patient has a large liver lying under the skin, she would enter it through the new hole as well."

"You've read Dr. Conway's deposition, right? And did you see her description of changing the angle of the needle at the repeated insertions?"

"Yeah. She may have done it, yeah."

"And that was acceptable to you, at least as far as using the same point in the skin?"

"If she would test where the tip of the needle is, but she didn't do any test."

"All right. And then she tries it the second time, read occluded again, didn't do any of the tests that you have just described, and that's a problem?"

"Big problem."

"She removes the needle and then tests to make sure it is patent. You don't have a problem with that, do you?"

"No. No problem here."

"And then she tries again."

"Yet again without testing."

"We just said it."

"Yeah. But this is the third time now."

"Well, I'm just—I'm trying to take it step by step by step," the defense lawyer says with his innocent smile.

Another silence. Furrer digs into his pile of papers. I wink at Veronica. She responds with a faint smile. Furrer looks up and opens his mouth. *Where is he going now?*

Doctor, in your 'Answers to Interrogations' it is phrased this way, and I want to know if this is your terminology or not or the lawyer's. It says that at this point Dr. Conway should have realized this same aggressive technique had failed twice already. Is the term 'aggressive' one that you used?"

What's the fuck? What is he talking about? I try to remember. Yes, at some stage of the lawsuit, a year or so ago, the defendants submitted a long list of questions to Veronica's law

firm. I was asked to help and reply to those questions. But the
lengthy legal document 'Answers to Interrogations' was produced
by the lawyers. I may have browsed briefly over it. It takes me
ten seconds to gather my thoughts.

"I would say obstinate, obstinate or wrong. Aggressive? You
can call it aggressive. I don't have any problem with this word."

"Well, you don't have any issue with it, but it wasn't your
word?"

"No, I didn't say aggressive. Or did I? I don't remember."
The bastard manages to fluster me.

"And doctor, here's what I hate to ask, because if it wasn't
your word, then you're trying to use someone else's descriptive
term. If it was your word, I'd like to know what you meant by
aggressive?"

I do not understand what Furrer is trying to achieve with this
irritating *lawyerspeak*. And I sound irritated when I reply: "You
see, I could use many different words to describe the repeated
attempts to insert the needle at the same spot. I could call it
inappropriate, or stupid or silly, or poor judgment. You want me
to continue?"

Furrer is calm as ever: "And all those terms to describe the
surgeon's decision to use the needle in the right upper quadrant?"

Oh' God, how many times he wants me to repeat myself.
"Yeah. And also she had chance to stop the first time, she had
chance to stop the second time, the third time, stop and think,
what's wrong, why I'm not successful. Maybe consult one of her
colleagues. She works in a large hospital, right? She could stop
and think. But she just went on and on, like, obsessed with the
need to go on with the operation, against all odds, which, I
believe, reflects very poor judgment."

"All right. Have you read anything that says that trying once,
twice, three times, reflects poor judgement?"

"Yes, I read a lot…". I tell him, yet again, that some people
say this and others say that; that in surgery there are options and
there is a spectrum to everything; that circumstances are different
and that doing it blindly and in the right upper quadrant was
wrong. "You live in Gulfport, right? So if you walk at night in
the streets of your small town you probably don't need to carry a
gun. But if you live, say in Bagdad or in in Kabul, you would
need to carry a gun with you all the time. So when working in

dangerous sites, such as the right upper quadrant, one has to be much more careful."

Furrer's next series of questions deal with the third insertion of the Veress needle. Why do I think the needle entered a vein, what would happen if that were an artery, what the difference; he brings in again the structure and function of the insufflating machine. His last question in this series: "So when Dr. Conway inserted the needle the third time the monitor read 20. What was that reading in your eyes?"

"It tells me that the pressure measured by the tip of the needle was 20 and this is not the spot you want your needle to be in. The pressure within the free peritoneal cavity, where you want your needle to be, is below 8 mm Mercury. If it's higher, you are in a wrong spot. As I said before, with such pressure most likely you are inside a vein."

"Doctor, in your 'Answers to Interrogations' you wrote: 'Dr. Conway failed to consider alternative diagnosis/or alternative action plans.' This statement is written in the point of time in the chronology where the third attempt is happening, the pressure has increased to 20, and the monitor reads occluded."

"Yes?"

"What was she supposed to do at that moment?"

"Well, the anesthetist told her that the blood pressure is down, I don't remember exactly what the measurements were, but the patient has a cardiac arrest. So she should have thought immediately about the likelihood that she's now dealing with air emboli. This entity should have been high on the list of things that could happen during insufflation of gas. And she should have immediately placed the patient in the left lateral decubitus position."

"But hold on Doctor. Didn't Dr. Conway act appropriately by abandoning the attempt to insufflate when the monitor read occluded?"

"It took six seconds for the monitor to read occluded." My voice in now tired. I feel drained. "Look, the case speaks for itself. The patient had air in the chambers of her heart, and the air did not come from blowing her nose. The air came through the Veress needle. *res ipsa loquitur.* Isn't this the term that you lawyers like to use? So why should we ask so many questions? We know what happened and why…"

"Well, I'm just trying to understand," the defense lawyer says laconically and continuous to chew the same piece of fat. After a few more questions to 'clarify the last question', he asks: "You think that the patient should have been properly repositioned to relieve the cardiac air lock? And you think that this should have been done immediately upon her condition changing?"

"Didn't I say it already?"

"Please answer the question doctor."

"Well, say you're a qualified surgeon. You are doing this operation. You are board certified. You have been attending update courses. You know about the dangers of air emboli. Now, you've seen the monitor reading 20. So now you realize immediately what is the problem and what to do—to put the patient on her left side. But she didn't do it…" I notice that I'm raising my voice and I may sound angry but I can help it. "She was lost, she didn't know what's happening. She lost control on the situation. So they are doing a code, all the experts come in and dance around the patient. And no one thinks about air emboli… as crucial time is passing."

"All right. So you believe that Dr. Conway should have immediately thought that this is air emboli?"

"Of course!" I want to scream with frustration. "Here she is pumping the abdomen with air and the patient collapses. Of course she should have thought about this."

After going on almost four hours, Mr. Furrer seems as fresh and persevering as ever. I know what will be his next move: to suggest that air emboli are extremely rare; if so, why should we expect the surgeon to consider such a rare condition? And indeed, he asks:

"Have you ever been in a procedure where this has happened?"

"Yes, somebody injected air into an i.v line, some nurse, the patient arrested. Died."

"You were present there or you have heard about it?"

"I was present."

"And other than the one case, have you ever been involved and even seen air emboli in any other surgical setting?"

"No, no personal experience. But from time to time one hears about such cases in one's own hospital, other surgeons, or elsewhere. You know, often such complications are hushed…".

"And you know that Mr. Gospel lived?"

"Good. Luckily!"

"Okay. I want to go down to page 16 of the 'answers to interrogations'. It says: 'According to Dr. Zohar, Dr. Conway performed an unnecessary laparotomy.' Why do you think it was unnecessary?"

"Because there was no need for it. Why did she have to open the abdomen? There was no gas in the peritoneal cavity—she never succeeded pumping any gas into it. So why add morbidity? Why cut and open the abdomen? No indication whatsoever."

Furrer never accepts any answer without asking the same question again: "So you wouldn't have done it?"

"Of course not. Especially not in this patient who is now in critical condition. Besides, there are other ways to find out if the patient has free gas in her tummy or not."

"For example?"

"There was an X ray machine in the room anyway. Just take a flat X ray of the abdomen. Takes 30 seconds."

"Okay. And how did the laparotomy add to the patient's morbidity?"

"Well, first it added to the postoperative pain. Second, she has been left with a large abdominal scar. Third, she may develop a hernia—which would be common in an obese patient. Fourth, she may suffer in the future intestinal obstruction caused by scarring, you know, the adhesions forming in the abdomen after any surgery. Any surgery, indicated or not, could cause complication one day."

"It could, but you've been provided with this patient's medical records. Have you seen any indication of any complication caused by that laparotomy?"

"Well, I didn't have any information about the patient after she recovered from this. I think that my job as expert witness on this case was to focus on the peri-operative events, before, during and immediately after the operation. No late developments. Likewise, I won't be going into her brain function—I'm not a brain expert..."

"You are not going to speak about her recovery?"

"No."

Furrer looks surprised. "So...all right. Let's take a break for a second." *A second. Fuck him. I need to eat something.* The videographer, about whom I have forgotten completely, says, "We are going off record at 1:07 pm."

I grab an apple from my backpack and walk into the corridor. Veronica follows me.

"When is he going to finish?" I ask.

"I think he is running out of questions. An hour or so, I suppose. When he's done I'll ask you a few. Won't take long. We have a flight to catch."

I return to my chair at the table. Furrer is skimming through his papers, a half chewed KitKat in his hand. Noticing me, he lifts his head. "You must be in a hurry to go back to work. We should be done in an hour or so."

I feel inclined to be nice to the guy. After all, he only doing his job. "So how is fishing in Gulport?" I ask.

"I don't fish. Not enough time for everything."

"So what do you do in your free time?"

"I organize youth orchestras, marching orchestras. We travel a lot across the country. Almost every weekend."

I want to ask more but the court clerk and Veronica are back.

15

"We are back on the record at 1:25," declares the videographer.

"All right Dr. Zohar," resumes the youth orchestra leader, "I've a couple of follow-up questions on things we've talked already. The two tests that we have mentioned, the saline drop test, what was the name of the other…"

"The aspiration test," I help him.

"Ah, all right. In what percentage are those tests accurate? Have you seen any studies talking about the accuracy?"

"I didn't look for such studies."

"I understand. Have you seen or read anything that questions the accuracy of the saline drop test and says it's not really necessary?"

"Yes. Some surgeons think that if they enter the abdomen in a safe spot, they don't need to waste time doing such tests. But nothing is hundred percent accurate in medicine or life. Things can fail. Tests can fail."

"And so you are aware that some writers, surgeons, have said that it's not necessary to do the saline drop test?"

"Yeah."

"And you disagree with them?"

"Not really. They think that they know what they are doing. They think that they know how inset the needle safely in a safe spot."

"So—".

"The first time, first time," I interrupt him.

"—you wouldn't do it that way?" Furrer manages to deliver his question.

"I wouldn't use Veress needle at all. Anyway, you're talking about the first attempt. But I'm talking about the second one, the third one."

"And it would be your understanding that what is being discussed in the literature about those tests applies to the first attempt?"

"Of course! Normal surgeons would not attempt re-insertion, again and again, at the same place without testing. Normal surgeons use common sense. We know that wearing a safety belt is common sense. We don't question it. Not everyone who drives a car without a safety belt will be injured. But he is more

likely to be injured if he doesn't wear a belt. The same in
surgery."

"You write a lot about common sense. In your books."

"Yeah." *Stop your phony flattering me.*

"But you agree that there are surgeons whose opinions and
practice concerning the use of the Veress needle differ from yours
and this doesn't mean that they are wrong or breach of the
standard of care. Correct?"

"Yes. In general, correct. But look. You see, most people
don't wear a parachute when they drive a car. But when they're
flying a jet fighter, they will wear a parachute. It's a different
story now. And you are mixing two stories—the story of
inserting a needle the first time in a safe spot versus a story doing
it again and again in a dangerous site—the right upper quadrant."

"And you may say that what we were discussing just now is
also true about the aspiration test. That there are some authors
who have questioned the accuracy and usefulness of this test?"

"Well, they don't question the fact that if you aspirate blood
into the syringe it's clear that you are in a blood vessel because
it's obvious. They don't use it because they think they know how,
and where, insert a needle without entering a blood vessel."

"Doctor, how old are you?"

"I'm sixty-five." *Here it comes.* Now, having exhausted me
for five hours, he will start to be "personal". They all do it to
some extent—some less, some more. I brace myself. I need to
force myself to be as superficially gracious as this benign looking
character. Suddenly an image of Mr. Furrer appears in my mind:
a dumpy, chubby, middle-aged man, clad in uniforms of the
confederate army, holding a conductor's baton, marching in front
of his ensemble. I suppress a giggle.

"And you still maintain a full surgical schedule?"

"Sure."

"And you have plans to slow that schedule down or step
down at some point?"

"Well, I'm a rural surgeon. So I'm not extremely busy, and
I'm doing fine. Maybe in four or five years I will retire. I think
that my skills, both mentally and physically, are well preserved.
So I continue."

"You have at least quoted others that at age sixty, the eyes
and hands start to fail you?"

I do not know what he's talking about. I have written so many things and do not know what he is quoting, whether what he quotes is accurate. But I have to reply:

"I don' remember this. Anyway, you know, each of us is different. Some fail early, some fail late. Some fail very late. At this stage, I don't see myself failing. I thank you for your concern."

"Okay. Let me ask you about some other things. We were talking about the time you were in Iowa." Furrer inquires about my brief Iowa sojourn and the much longer one in New York. He does it very gently, sounding almost sympathetic: what were the issues with my partner in Iowa? The nature of my struggle against the so called "Irani Mafia" at the Episcopalian Hospital in Brooklyn? Why did I leave my final New York position at the Bronx Riverside Hospital? I answer laconically to all his questions.

He picks up a paper from the top of his pile and hands it to me. "Doctor, do you recognize it?"

I see the logo of the New York Times at the top. "Sure, this is an article which describes exactly what we were talking about."

"But the article says that you have been fired. Whereas just an hour ago you stated that you have never lost or surrendered your privileges".

"And I never…the CEO at the Episcopalian Hospital wrote a letter of termination. You see, he was blackmailed to do so by the Iranians who controlled the Medical Board. But a day after the New York Times article had been published he had rescinded his letter."

"So why did you leave the Episcopalian?"

"I left almost a year later. The atmosphere was poisoned. I wanted to move on. A small golden parachute helped."

The defense lawyer pauses, as if lost in thoughts, for a few moments. I play with my pen and stare at the celling. I feel apathetic, like an infantryman under constant and endless artillery barrage. The allegory, when it comes to my mind, is ridiculous: some 44 years ago, I was lying for many hours, with my head buried in the deep Sinai sand, while Egyptian, Soviet-made bombs were falling all around me. I survived. I tell myself: dealing with this asshole means nothing to me.

Furrer interrupts my daydream. "I want to change the subject a little. In your book "Common Myths in Surgery, that's one of your books, right?"

"Not a book. It was an article."

"And are there any of those common myths that you think applicable to this case?"

I think fast. What is he up to? There were a hundred myths listed in that article. "Well, let me have a copy of the article. I'll look through it and hopefully I'll be able to answer your question."

Furrer's right hand searches through his pile of papers. "I don't know if I have a copy with me but I might. I think that Ms. Chapman knows that No. 47 on your list of common myths, for example, would be applicable."

Veronica leaps up from her chair. "I'm going to object to this line of questioning because I haven't seen what you're referring to or talking about."

Furrer looks at her calmly. "Okay. You haven't looked at his webpage?" Like a teacher reprimanding a pupil for not doing her homework.

"I mean I haven't seen this particular article. I have seen the webpage." She appears apologetic.

"Oh' I found it," Furrer announces. "Here it is. Item 47: "Diagnostic laparoscopy decreases the incidence of negative appendectomies.""

"Well, this is a well-known myth. What has it to do with the case under discussion?" I cannot hide my contempt.

"Oh well. I just used that item as an example. It may be that it was not number 47 that caught my eyes. Here, please look at the list of the myths and tell me whether you think any item is relevant?"

I pretend reading the document. I know that no item on the list is pertinent, but I take my time. Let him wait. After a minute, I drop the paper on the table. "Nothing relevant, Sir."

"Right. What about your other publications? Here is a copy of your CV. Anything that you've authored that has a direct relationship to the allegations in this case?"

"No. I never wrote any article dealing specifically with air emboli or the use of the Veress needle. But I edited a book about surgical complications and it includes chapters on the prevention and management of complications associated with laparoscopic procedures."

To conclude, Furrer asks a series of leading questions which require me to declare, yet again, that "no", I haven't used the Veress needle since 1995, that "no", I have never treated air embolism in person; and that, "yes"—air emboli are extremely rare.

"I have no more questions," Furrer says. He immediately starts stowing papers into his suitcase. It is 2:30 afternoon.

The plaintiff attorney now takes over. "Doctor. I'd like to go back to the laparotomy surgery that Mr. Furrer asked you about. And you said that you weren't quite sure if you would say that that was a breach of the standard of care. But wouldn't you agree with me that that was an unnecessary surgery?"

"Yes," I say.

"Object to the form," Furrer interjects.

Veronica ignores him: "Would you agree with me that performing a surgery on a patient unnecessarily is a breach of the standard of care?"

"Object to the form," Furrer repeats. Calmly. He never raises his voice.

"You can answer," Veronica tells me.

"He's already—he's already answered that question—" says Furrer.

"You can answer," repeats Veronica. Her face flushed.

I open my mouth to reply but Furrer interferes: "—Well, if he's going to change his opinion, he'll answer it."

"No," I answer, "I can't change my opinion because that was a question of fine judgement, under difficult circumstances and not everything we do can be defined as black or white; there is a gray zone in between. And there are situations for which we simply do not know what the standard of care is, or might be. In certain situations, like the one we are discussing, you have a few seconds to think, to decide. And you are stressed, things happen fast, you know. So it was unnecessary, yes. But I can't talk about deviation from the standard of care because there's no standard of care for this situation."

Veronica is stubborn. "And even if that—even if the laparotomy increased her morbidity, as you had testified to before, wouldn't you agree that it would be a breach of the standard of care."

Why is she now arguing with me, trying to change my mind? An experienced lawyer going into a deposition should have pre-agreed with her expert witness on each and every item to be discussed. She should have known my opinion on any question pertinent to the case.

Apparently Mr. Furrer things the same: "Objection to trying to get this counsel's witness to change his prior testimony."

Veronica, ignoring Furrer, looks at me: "Do you have a remark?"

"No. I can't add to what I said."

Veronica takes a deep breath. It is not easy for this young gal to oppose an old fox like Furrer. "Doctor, you talked today about several breaches of the standard of care. Correct?"

"Yes, yes." I look at my watch openly. Enough is enough, I want to go home.

"Okay. And is it your opinion that the breaches caused her anoxic brain injury?"

"Yes. Of course."

Veronica consults her notes. "I just want to talk just a little bit about whether or not the actual surgery, the initial decision to operate on the hernia was a breach in the standard of care. You have stated that you needed to review additional records, specifically the surgeon's office encounter with Mrs. Gospel. But I just want you to assume for a fact that if Mrs. Gospel was not complaining of any pain, she had no other complaints, if there was no indication that she was going to have any sort of intestinal strangulation, would it be your opinion that the hernia surgery was a breach in the standard of care?"

Yet again, I have to disappoint the plaintiff's lawyer. "You see, the spectrum of standard of care is very wide. And the patient's wishes need to be included. So if the patient wanted her hernia to be fixed, even if the hernia was asymptomatic, then it's OK to do so. But my point is this: the patient should have been told that it is OK not to operate on an asymptomatic hernia. That not all hernias have to be fixed. We don't know whether this has been mentioned to her by the surgeon."

"Okay. I think those are all the questions that I have."

Great. Finally. I jump up, ready to gather my things. But Furrer is not finished. He shoves back across the table the few documents he had borrowed from me to examine.

"There are a couple of pages, there's some notes. This is the copy of the deposition of Dr. Conway. What did you mean with the question mark on page five?"

"Oh, when asked whether the trans-esophageal echo is an immediate test she said it's done bedside. So, how can it be an immediate test? You have to summon the expert, get the machine, inert the tube into the esophagus. It takes time. Twenty minutes. Half an hour."

"And do you know how long it took in this case?"

"No. We don't know. She didn't want to say."

"Okay. And what is this?" Furrer points to another page of Conway's deposition. "Did you write here a BS?"

"Sure. I thought that her justification to open the abdomen was BS."

"Hopefully, Doctor, it's not—oh, yes, one more BS." I'm not sure whether Furrer is amused or pretends to be scandalized.

"Yes, it is BS." I explain why.

Furrer: "All right. That's all."

Everyone stands up. The table is being cleared.

I say: "Six hours, Mr. Furrer. I was paid for a 3-hour deposition.

Furrer pretends he does not hear me. "Don't worry," says Veronica, "they'll pay."

To reach the door I had to go around the table where Furrer was still busy organizing his things. I stopped and shook his hand: "I enjoyed meeting you Sir."

Furrer turned around: "My pleasure doctor. We'll see you again in a few months in court, in Biloxi. I bet you will enjoy our warm sun in December." An earnest smile.

I smiled back and went out of the door. *Court, what court?* How are they going to defend all those allegations? Where would they find an expert to shield a surgeon who had committed a chain of errors, which had permanently damaged the plaintiff? Anyway, where on earth is Biloxi?

Outside, a cool breeze was steering the spring tree leaves. I stood on the curb with Veronica, awaiting her airport taxi, relishing the soft afternoon sun. Veronica reassured me that "you did well". I felt good as well—sensing that I had delivered a clear message. We chatted a bit. Which, from my experience with business-like lawyers, usually means, that I ask the questions and they answer. I asked her about her relationship with Dwight Browning—the senior partner.

"Oh', I work for him in Gulfport. I'm not licensed in Louisiana, you see, only in Mississippi. Our main office is in New Orleans. This is where Dwight sits. He's a great lawyer. But I'm afraid we are going to lose him soon. He's running for election to the State's Supreme Court. He wants to be a supreme judge. He's quite serious about it."

A dilapidated cab, a 1990's Crown Vic, appeared screeching in front of us.

"So what do you think," I asked Veronica while helping with her luggage, "are they going to settle?"

"Not so fast," she replied, "defense always take their time—as long as they work on the case they make money—lots of it. Bye now."

"Take care," I replied. I was hopeful that I would never see her or Furrer ever again. I climbed onto my red F-105 and sailed northward.

16

I was surprised when, a month later, the defense disclosed its expert witness. I immediately recognized his name: Dr. Timothy F. Hutchinson. The famous hernia surgeon. A star. Didn't I attend his lecture at the American College of Surgeons meeting a few years ago? Very impressive. Why would a guy like this agree to defend such problematic case? I wondered.

In his lengthy "defendant's expert disclosure" Mr. Furrer stated that Dr. Hutchinson will testify that everything—point by point and item by item—committed by the defendant surgeon was within the standard of care; that Dr. Hutchinson will refute all the allegations laid out by the Plaintiff. *Really?* I was amazed.

I knew that Hutchinson is considered a big shot in the field of hernia surgery—especially laparoscopic hernia surgery. But I had to learn more about him—online and sniffing around. What I found was a poster boy of American Surgery: the best college in the Deep South, a leading local medical school, the top ivory tower surgical training; a laparoscopic fellowship in a renowned Mid-Western center; an author of a decent number of publications (more than 400) and of a few books. At his current University Hospital in Florida, he had developed a dedicated *Hernia Center*. I read on the hospital webpage, "Dr. Hutchinson has guided his team to become one of the most recognized surgical units in the country, performing thousands of complex surgical procedures for patients from this region as well as more than 30 other states and countries." I also read that, "He is a world-renowned surgeon who lectured in six continents". Cleary, one of the guys—I knew in person a few of such characters— "who flies around the world, shows great slides and is known by everybody and everywhere…"

Yes, doctors and especially surgeons are not known to suffer of excessive modesty (modesty is not good for business): whenever one goes one hears about "our internationally famous local surgeon". But in Hutchinson's case this was not fake commercial propaganda—my buddies in South Africa and South America and India and Europe all knew about him; many having attended his lectures in Mumbai, Acapulco or Rome.

On the many pictures of Hutchinson available on "google images", I saw a good-looking man in his late 40's or early 50's. Tall, thin, square faced, smiling. And indeed, on one of those "online chats", where patients use to share their experiences, a woman wrote: "The first time I saw Dr. Hutch I was impressed how handsome he is..." Another ex-patient described his fantastic bedside manners—"a charmer". On his twitter account, I found how he describes himself: "Father, Teacher, Runner, Fisherman; Chief-Gastrointestinal and Minimally Invasive Surgery; Director-Florida Hernia Center."

Why then is this surgical star, this good old Southern Boy, taking on himself the defense of Dr. Conway, I asked myself. Does he know her in person, having met her in one of his laparoscopic hernia courses? Was he one of her mentors? Is one of her current colleagues a buddy of his? Does she refer to him her complex cases and complications? Any of these possibilities sounded plausible: after all, the "southern surgical community" must be a tightly knitted club, its members loyal to each other. This is why the plaintiff's expert witness had to be recruited from far away.

I looked up Dr. Hutchinson's ('Hutch" to his friends) legal activities. The search was productive: he had an extensive record of expert witness activities—for the defense, never on the plaintiff's side. In one of such cases, I read, Dr. Hutchinson's role was not to testify about the clinical merits of the litigation but to help the defense to discredit the qualifications, the expertise, of the opposing expert. The litigating lawyer commented: "We find Dr. Hutchinson's answer troubling because he did not merely state his understanding of whether the expert for the plaintiffs is qualified to testify but went further and appeared to speak on behalf of the surgical organization, which he is not formally representing". In another highly cited case, Hutchinson testified in defense of a giant medical device company, sued for complications associated with the hernia-mesh it had produced and marketed. The company lost.

Another legal case involving Hutchinson was juicier. The court records told the entire story. When working as a consultant for another medical device company Hutchinson engaged in a prolonged affair with a company employee. It appeared that he shared a sexually transmitted disease with her. As the disease had been described to be "surgically removed", I gathered it must have been "genital warts". To cut the story short: after a year or so Hutch dumped the woman. When she started bad-mouthing him to her colleagues, she was told to shut up. Eventfully she was terminated. She sued company for discrimination, and lost. This was some ten years ago; different times, I thought; these days she may have won. *So the poster boy is adventurous*, I smiled to myself.

Surely, I thought, a guy like this, who must be making more than a million bucks a year, does not need to engage in legal work for money. Is he doing it for fun? Perhaps, successfully defending local surgeons could contribute to his reputation and popularity.

Now I examined myself—the expert on the other side. What I saw was the opposite of the All American Surgical Hero: almost twenty years older, shorter, not so good looking, a foreign accent, and less eloquent. Moreover, much less famous and with a CV tainted by foreign education and career. In Hollywood's terms, Hutchinson's image against mine could be compared to that of Harrison Ford's versus Woody Allen's. Who of those two would appear, I asked myself, more authoritative, more convincing, and more "surgical"? That is, not in Williamsburg, Brooklyn but in the Deep South.

However, while aware of the obvious difficulties, I felt challenged. Let me go, I thought, and confront him. Let me try convincing the Jury. I appreciated the Jury system. I hoped that a Jury of common citizen—in our case it would help to include a few blacks—would be fair. That they would possess some common sense, and be sympathetic to the injured party. I hoped that they will not be overly impressed by the "big town smoothly taking expert", that they may feel for the other expert—who talks in plain language— persuading them that the harm inflicted on the plaintiff could have been prevented.

I prepared myself. I read everything relevant to our case that the great Dr. Hutchinson has written. This included a book chapter in which he had advocated using the Palmer point as the site of the preferred initial abdominal entry with the Veress needle.

I found a paper he had co-authored in 2004, describing a patient undergoing laparoscopic cholecystectomy. A Veress needle had been placed in the right upper quadrant to initiate abdominal access. Shortly after insufflation of the gas, the patient developed cardiovascular collapse. The gas insufflation was immediately stopped and the patient placed in the Durant position. She stabilized quickly, and the procedure was continued successfully. In the discussion section of the paper, the authors admitted the error of inserting the needle in the right upper quadrant and emphasized the importance of early recognition of air emboli, and immediate placement of the patient in left lateral position as the most important life saving measure. They concluded: "Carbon dioxide embolism during laparoscopy, albeit rare, can be a fatal complication of the procedure. Whenever sudden changes in hemodynamic stability occur, venous gas embolism should be considered. The general surgeon must be aware of this entity."

I found yet another publication coauthored by Hutchinson. It described a patient who developed air emboli during open chest surgery for trauma. In that case, the air emboli were missed and the patient died. The authors concluded: "Regardless of the etiology of air embolus, a high index of suspicion as well as rapid and aggressive treatment is crucial to reduce the chance of death. The management algorithm includes prevention of further entry of air, changes in patient positioning…"

Avoidance of the right upper quadrant, using the Palmer point, early recognition, change of position. This is what Hutch himself had recommended, I thought. This is what Conway failed to do. And now he wants to defend her?

I warned Veronica that Hutchinson is a "big fish"—a formidable opponent. I shared with her whatever material I managed to dig about him and suggested how to use it during his cross-examination, or even better, during his deposition. "Are you guys going to depose him?" I asked.

Her answer was negative. I was not surprised. While the well-funded defense team tends to depose everyone on the planet, the plaintiff's team, working on contingency basis, counts each cent. A pity, I thought. I could advise them on how to trim Hutchinson's wings already at his deposition. Oh' well, I thought, let us hope they will know how to deal with him at court. With their help, and in front of the jury, I could be their David — slaying Goliath.

With the dates for the trial in Biloxi, Mississippi, established for December, the defense lawyer dedicated the month of

November to compose lengthy motions ("supported" with numerous citations from statutes and my deposition) for "summary judgement", calling to disqualify me as an expert witness. Mr. Furrer wrote:

"The expert testimony must be grounded in methods and procedures of science, not merely a subjective belief or unsupported speculation. The Adventist Hospital is filing this motion for summary judgement for the following grounds: the plaintiff's liability expert lacks sufficient familiarity with the technique and instruments used by Dr. Conway in performing the surgery in question. He also does not have any experience in the diagnosis and management of the complication occurring in this case. Therefore, he lacks the qualifications and experience to testify as an expert in this case. In the absence of competent expert testimony the plaintiff's medical malpractice claim must fail."

I wrote to Veronica: "The defense lawyer claims that I have admitted that I have no personal experience in the management of air emboli—which, I admit, is a very rare complication. He asks how I can serve as an expert on this case. The parallel would be a pilot of an airliner who has never experienced a disaster in the air — which is an extremely rare event. Surely, both the pilot and the surgeon should be trained to recognize all potential (rare) complications and deal with them promptly. Any pilot has to know what to do when suddenly both engines die. Likewise, any surgeon has to know how to deal with air embolism during laparoscopic procedures."

We countered the motion with a lengthy Affidavit. The motion was dismissed by the Judge. He agreed that I am qualified to provide testimony in this case. I was going to Biloxi.

PART 4: THE COURT IN BILOXI

17

On an early December day, I unearthed a blue blazer. Years ago, when I moved to the country, I donated all my New York suits to Goodwill. I searched for a pair of trousers to match. A pair of relatively new Walmart black jeans was my only option. This would be all right, I thought, the jury will not mind.

At the Twin Cities' airport, awaiting the flight to New Orleans, I googled up Dwight Browning —Veronica's senior partner—with whom I would be meeting later in the afternoon in Biloxi. I had spoken with him only once on the phone; Veronica told me about his run for the State Supreme Court, but otherwise I knew nothing about him. What I learned was this:

"Educated in Louisiana and Mississippi (*Cum Laude);* practices medical malpractice and severe and catastrophic personal injuries for more than thirty years; this includes complex catastrophic injury cases such as those involving birth asphyxia/ hypoxic ischemic encephalopathy, traumatic brain injury, and spinal cord injury; has considerable expertise in the field of maritime and admiralty laws; has extensive courtroom experience, including the United States Supreme Court; Mr. Browning's efforts on behalf of his clients have yielded numerous seven-figure results, including recoveries of $12.4 million, $9.25 million, $6 million, $4.055 million, $3.03 million, $2.27 million, and $1.5 million."

The senior partner's picture on the webpage showed a serious looking, bespectacled white haired man; around sixty, I thought. I wondered why such an accomplished litigator is bothering to be personally involved in this humble case. I was curious to meet him, see him in action.

As I climbed on the Boeing 737 to New Orleans everything what I had planned to say, how I would act in front the jury, was ready in my brain—what was left to study was the list of restaurants in Biloxi.

The ride eastwards, from New Orleans to Biloxi, along the coastal highway 10 took eighty minutes. Turning the car radio on you knew that you are in the Deep South: country music, gospel, black or white preachers; or, even worse, one of those crazy ultra-conservative talk shows—rough male voices disseminating rage and hate.

Biloxi, Mississippi. A previously dormant, little fishing town has been transformed over the years: clusters of monstrous casino-hotels were built along the beach, blocking the sea away from the town. I parked the rented Chevy Silverado pickup in front of a huge casino-hotel and handed it to a Valet Parking attendant. Although I had pre-booked an economy rental car in New Orleans this pickup was the only vehicle readily available at Avis.

I checked in the casino-hotel—a "white elephant". An immense pseudo-majestic lobby, permeated with artificial vanilla scent, connected to the never-ending casino complex. The thick carpets, the colors, the marble, the plants, suggested a tacky imitation of the Taj Mahal of Bombay. Five-star exterior and interior for the price of a three-star —to attract the gambling plebs. And the plebs — herds of them, mainly the lower classes and the retirees—flocking in droves from all over the South—to enjoy the illusion, at least for a few days, of living the high life; to gain, or loose, the meagre social security income on which they survive.

I settled in a spacious room on the thirty-third floor overlooking the Gulf of Mexico—blue, flat and empty, the winter sun setting down. *Shit, no mini-bar*—they want you to drink downstairs at the casino and gamble. I changed into shorts and a T-shirt and went down for a few refreshing laps in the pool overlooking the ocean. An Olympic-size, heated pool that was completely deserted. People come here to gamble and eat and drink and gamble — not to swim. I saw many octogenarians; the younger ones were predominantly overweight —some significantly morbidly obese. In the elevator, I noted a couple of fatties in double-size wheelchairs pushed by their wives or partners. A few had an oxygen tank attached to the wheel chair.

I was scheduled to meet with the lawyers for a final pre-trial discussion at 5 pm. Back in my room, I showered, dried up and changed back to shorts and T-shirt. I was starving and thirsty, but this will have to wait. I swallowed the last few almonds left in my backpack and descended to the lobby.

Already from faraway, I recognized Veronica, standing near the reception desk. In her white-yellow pantsuit and high heels, she merged well into the surroundings. Coming closer I noted the heavy make-up. She seemed a little chubbier since we had met during the deposition.

"Hello Doc, welcome to Biloxi," she smiled pleasantly, "hope you have travelled well."

"Dwight," she referred to Browning, the senior partner, "will meet us up in his suite, it would be quieter there." She led me through long corridors into a separate hotel tower reserved for "special" guests—the frequent fliers and high-end gamblers. On the way, she maintained small talk: "From Gulfport to Biloxi, it's only half an hour ride. We often come here for a show. Yes, we stay overnight. No, we don't gamble. Great restaurants in the casino. Some great food in town as well."

At the entrance to the VIP tower, we had to pass through a security checkpoint, where Veronica displayed her resident card. We entered the private elevator that took us to the top floor. The elevator opened directly into the suite's vast lounge, where Mr. Browning was waiting. He looked his age, around the sixties. The years on the golf course, on an ocean going yacht, must have been unkind to his face. Medium height, slim, in a white, slightly crumbled shirt. I noticed the dark suit jacket and necktie disorderly hanging on a dining table chair.

"Hi there, doctor, thanks for coming." A swift, weak, functional handshake. He led us to a sitting area at the corner of the room, overlooking the ocean—same view like from my room, but a different perspective. "Please sit down."

While he was fiddling with a little suitcase, retrieving out some files, I eyed with concealed nostalgia the mini-bar at the side of the room. After the flight, the drive, the long swim, I was dreaming about a cold frosty beer. However, business like, Browning went directly to work, not even offering a glass of water.

The meeting was brief, no more than forty-five minutes. He ran the case over with me. "Your job is the operation, what's in the operative report. Veronica will be the one to examine you and you know what to say—exactly what you've said at the deposition. Simple, eh? Mr. Furrer will then cross-examine you.

Just stick to your points. Don't let him confuse you. We'll start tomorrow morning, nine am. But you'll take the stand later, perhaps even after lunch, after I'm finishing cross-examining the surgeon. Yes, we'll start the morning with the surgeon's testimony. She's mine. I'll deal with her. By then the Judge will be well prepared to absorb your opinion."

"When is their expert, Dr. Hutchinson's turn? When will he appear?" I asked.

"Oh, only the day after tomorrow, in the morning, on Friday."

I unzipped my rucksack. "I brought with me a few papers published by Hutchinson. I thought you might want to discuss them. I believe Veronica has them already. I sent it to her but never heard how you guys intend using these papers against him. I think these papers could help you…"

The senior partner raised his hand impatiently. "No need. Leave Hutchinson to me. The more academic they are, the better are their qualifications on paper—the easier prey they are. I know how to deal with guys like this!"

I looked at Veronica. She was nodding enthusiastically. Like a girl scout listening to the chief of boy scouts at the jamboree, I thought.

"What about jury selection" I asked, "when will this take place?"

"Oh, no jury in this case," Browning replied gazing at the empty, darkening ocean way below us. I could see a few clouds gathering at the horizon.

"What? No jury? How come?" I was surprised and disappointed. *Why didn't they tell me? I was expecting a jury.* In my mind, based on my limited experience, a jury composed by layperson, of common citizen, is usually "fair" and looks favorably on a humble rural surgeon like me, regardless them being southerners and me a strange transplant from up north.

Browning continued gazing at the ocean as if trying to locate a single boat, or a ship, something I had not seen since my arrival. "According to the State rules, malpractice cases originating in a public hospital are litigated in front of a Judge. No jury," he explained laconically.

"Why?"

"Because the Adventist is a community hospital. Cases against hospitals like this are tried before a circuit judge without a jury, pursuant to the Mississippi Tort Claims Act."

Sure, I thought, they suppress their blacks' rights to vote. So why shouldn't they deprive them of the right for a fair trial before a jury of their peers?

I did not react but asked: "For how much money you are suing"

The senior partner waved his hand contemptuously, "Only half a million. The State has a cap. Such cases are hardly worth our time."

Then, he seemed to lose interest in me. "OK, doctor, we'll see you tomorrow at the court house. You know where it is?"

"Sure, I will be there." I knew where the courthouse was—at the heart of Biloxi's old center, a ten minutes stroll from the Casino. This was the same court featured in a few of John Grisham's fictional cases.

"Last question," I said with a smile, before I was pushed out of the door, "any place you would recommend for dinner?" I had already sensed that I will have to dine alone, but—who knows— perhaps the kind Veronica would offer to join me. I hate to eat alone, sitting at a bar, watching Fox News or some silly football game.

Suddenly, Browning came back to life and looked at me. Apparently, culinary matters were more interesting than this legal case. "Well, you have two options—the best place in town is the "French Old House" but the "Half Shell Oyster House" is not bad. Unless you want to try one of the Casino restaurants. Good night, doctor." The private elevator arrived. Veronica waved at me. The elevator's doors closed, I was going down. What will they do now, the two of them? *Will they, finally, open the mini bar?*

I left the "top litigator" with a budding notion that he has no human interest whatever in me: he wants me to spill out what I have to say and disappear from his face. I also started suspecting that this case is "small on him"—not worth spending too much time on the preparation of the witness—the person on whom hinges the outcome. A third of the half million would translate to something under two hundred thousand to his office—minus all the expenses—leaving perhaps enough to fuel his ocean going yacht. That is if we win. I trusted that Browning wants to win, otherwise what is the purpose of all this effort.

Early evening. The ocean now black as pitch. Somewhere, far away, a single light was blinking. A lighthouse? I changed into a pair of jeans and a light hoody. I grabbed my pipe, a small tin of pipe tobacco, a Swiss Army pocketknife, a credit card, and left the room. In the lobby, people were already standing in a long que, wheel chairs included, in front of the buffet restaurant. "Eat as much as you can for 25.99"—"including lobster tails"—the sign announced. Drinks not included. I strolled through the hotel's casino. I saw people pulling vigorously on the slot machines, a cigarette in mouth, and a drink in hand. Behind the gambling area, I spotted the restaurants: a posh steak house— caviar and lobsters on the side; exotic pan-Asian cuisine; coastal seafood and brew; Italian. All expensive and sterile, and half- empty. I longed for some fresh air and authenticity.

I crossed the busy Beach Boulevard and strolled into town. Coming down from Wisconsin I was cheered by the pleasant cool but mild breeze coming from the sea. The downtown, actually a little touristy village: a few colonial buildings, closed shops and offices, here and there a few bars and restaurants, glistering like small boats on a dark sea. I located the Oyster House. I was placed on a high chair at the counter, watching the oysters seething on the grill—a single man does not deserve a table in a busy restaurant. I had a few grilled oysters, a superb piece of grilled snapper, all washed down with two glasses of Malbec.

I took a walk along the seaside on a boardwalk beyond the line of casino-hotels. The wind grew stronger. A black man dragging a supermarket cart behind. Desolate.

I returned to the Casino around eight o'clock. The night was young. I wandered through the half-mile long gambling rooms— now more people at the slot machines, at the gambling tables, drinking and smoking and drinking. Tired looking, yawning casino employees. A sad and depressing scene. What is left to do for a lonely man? Go up to the room and read? But there was nothing to drink in the room. By now, my subconscious was hyped up, running the script for the court case of the next morning. I could feel already the adrenalin. The one and only option left was the bar.

I chose one of the bars in the center of the casino. A band of three was playing in the corner, their blond vocalist singing some popular oldies. I ordered a Johnny Walker, Red, with soda, thanks, no ice. I looked around the bar: mostly older couples, retirees?—heavily made up women sucking on long cocktails, men nursing tall beers. Everybody seemed to be puffing greedily on their cigarettes. On the other side of the bar, I spotted a gay couple, sharing a bottle of bubbly. The Scotch arrived, in a large glass, full to the brim. I tasted it—more whiskey than water. Only five bucks. I appraised at least a quarter bottle of whiskey in the glass. They are very generous with booze.

I passed my credit card to the barman. "Open a tab?" he asked. "Yes, why not."

I saw ashtrays all around the bar with an attached sign "Please no cigars." I took out the pipe from my pocket, extracted the tobacco tin from the other and packed the pipe with the strong, natural, dark, slow burning Cypriot Latakia flake tobacco. I lighted up, puffing vigorously, blowing blue dense clouds into the air. I was expecting some disapproval but the bar personnel ignored the smoke screen. An old woman sitting on my right leaned towards me and shouted—the music was loud—"oh' it smells so good. It reminds me of my father; he used to smoke a pipe." I took a long swig from the whiskey. Yum. I started feeling good.

"Where are you from?" the old lady tried to develop a conversation. "I'm Jennifer, this one is Harvey. We are from Texas, Galveston." She pointed to a man, wearing a cowboy hat, seating on her other side, with a Bud Light in his hand.

"I'm Mark. From Wisconsin."

"Nice to meet you, Mark." She smiled, exposing a decent set of teeth. "You have a cute accent. Doesn't sound to me a Wisconsin one."

Actually, I thought, she may be younger than I am. We ageing men tend to view ourselves young forever. "I'm originally from Israel," I replied.

"Ah. Israel. We love Israel. Harvey, listen, this gentleman here is from Israel!" Like many Southerners, she pronounced Israel as Is-rye-ell. Irritating.

"Thanks," I replied. I assessed my glass. Time for a re-fill?

The Texan carried on: "We adore Israel. We admire your President Bibi. And what do you think about Trump? He's going to be our next President, replacing that horrible Muslim. Trump's a great supporter of Israel."

Enough of that, I thought. "Actually, I'm not a fan of prime-minister Netanyahu. Nor that of candidate Trump." I tried to smile kindly at her and then looked away. End of conversation.

Sipping and puffing, I forced myself to rehearse the case for tomorrow. Do not forget the insufflator, I thought. Tell them that even when you block the gas tubing it takes five seconds until the monitor reads "occluded". During the long 5 seconds lots of CO_2 is pumped into the patient. Enough to kill her.

"Another drink?" asked a pretty bargirl. The bar was now crowded, with people standing all around. "Sure. The same please." Why not? What's the heck? Why not enjoy myself. I felt very good. I felt strong and ready for the battle. Perhaps like a character from one of John Grisham's novel seeking "justice" against the forces of dark evil.

The band was playing country. Two middle aged, stout women in cowboy boots were dancing around the bar. The Is-rye-ell loving couple joined them, clumsily performing line-dancing steps. I sipped slowly. *This will be your last drink.*

A young gal climbed on the vacant barstool on my right. Dark hair in a ponytail. Snub nose. Medium size but slim. Tight jeans. A hoodie top with a "University of Mississippi" logo. Cowboy boots. Not too much make up. In sum—cute. She ordered a Bud Light and lighted a cigarette, staring at the rows of bottles on the counter. A college girl? What is she doing here alone?

She kept smoking, imbibing slowly from her beer, looking straight ahead. I stole a glance or two at her. What I was seeing has become suddenly appetizing. I could feel, or I must have been imagining, the radiating warmth of her body. I have to go, I will leave in a minute or two, I told myself. Meanwhile I paid attention to my pipe. With the pocket knife I emptied the ash into an ashtray. I refilled the pipe with fresh tobacco from the tin. I re-lighted.

Lifting her bottle, her right elbow brushed against my arm, as by an accident.

"Sorry," she said. What a beautiful and innocent smile. Smiling blue eyes too. I could feel that long forgotten sensation of young flirts, dark bars, slow music. I needed another Scotch.

"You glass is empty, would you have another one?" she asked. Not waiting for reply, she called the barman, "Hey Jack, the same for this gentleman. The usual for me."

She's a regular. Who is she?

"It's on me," I signaled the barman, "add to the tab."

Now, with my third Johnny Walker on board, with the college girl sipping from some pink cocktail, I felt the beginning of a meltdown. As through a dense fog I learned that her name is Sheila. I must have engaged in some chitchat with her. Glasses were refilled yet again. She put her hand on my arm. Did she? I cannot remember for sure.

Early morning I woke up with a burning thirst. I could feel my parched tongue glued to the roof of the mouth. My head exploded with pain, spinning all around. I realized that I am back in my hotel room, lying, fully dressed, including shoes, on the made bed. *What happened?* I remembered the bar. Where is my credit card? Here, in my pocket. So I wasn't robbed. The court case, the bloody headache, I have to get up!

I swallowed two ibuprofens and one Tylenol. My heart was racing. This was always the case when I drink too much. I didn't remember myself so drunk since the wild residency years. I stood at the window, drinking water and looking out: the sea was lighting up, still dull and empty except a few clouds. Three hours left before the court. I was hoping that the hangover would lift up rapidly.

I played in my mind the events at the bar last night—why did I have to drink so much? Because of that cute girl? Surely not a college girl but a hooker. I am out of practice, I thought, not able to recognize a modern, concealed hooker. In this part of the world, prostitution is not legal—hence the hooker looks like a college girl. Some twenty years ago, things would have ended differently. How did I resist taking her to my room, this I could not remember, let alone how did I return to my room? I smiled to myself: imagine the police catching me with a hooker on the eve of my appearance in court. Imagine the headlines in the local newspapers.

I went down for a few laps in the pool, showered, dressed up. I looked at the mirror: the old black jeans to go along the blazer. This will do. With no jury to scrutinize you, you do not need to dress like a frikin' lawyer. A breakfast at the lobby's café. I

ordered a bowl of hot oatmeal—a portion which would satisfy a
working horse—to justify the 10.99 bill, including a pot of coffee.

18

8:45. I crossed the coastal highway and walked towards the Harrison County Courthouse of Biloxi. John Grisham mentioned Biloxi and its courthouse as a background for a few of his legal thrillers. The plot of the *The Runaway Jury* was set in Biloxi in the mid-1990s, portraying a lawsuit against tobacco companies. Grisham wrote, "The simple environment of the Biloxi courthouse allows for much of the action, as it has never held such a high-profile case..."

To my surprise the courthouse on the Martin Luther King, Jr. Boulevard proved to be a modest, relatively modern, two stories structure—not an old colonial house one would have expected in a historical Mississippi town.

I passed through the security and the metal detector. I had to leave my cell phone at the front office. I climbed up to the second floor and entered the courtroom through the main back door, leading into an empty public gallery. *Well, today's case is a law-profile one...*

I walked down the stairs and took a sit just behind the dividing bar. Down below I saw the two legal teams already settled in their places. The defense team by a table to the left of the Judge's bench. I noticed my old friend Mr. Furrer. He saw me, smiled and waved his hand. Two women sat at his table—a hospital lawyer? An insurance company lawyer? On the other side, just below me, I saw "our" team—Mr. Browning and Mrs. Chapman, Veronica. A younger attractive, blond woman was sitting with them. Later on I learned that she was Browning's paralegal. At the far end of the plaintiff's table sat another woman: black, obese, in her late 40's, dressed in an old, fading, hooded track suit, she seemed to be staring blankly into the space. She must be the plaintiff—the patient, I assumed.

Veronica sighted my arrival. She stood up and approached the bar. "Good morning Doctor, everything OK? If you need water, there's a vending machine in the corridor. It takes only dollar bills. Listen, there is an unexpected delay—Mr. Furrer has filed this morning another motion, yes, again disputing your qualifications as an expert. This will be the first item. I'm afraid your turn on the stand won't be up before afternoon."

Hell, and I believed that this—the issue of my qualifications—has been settled. It will be a long day. I hoped that I would survive into the afternoon. It could be nice to have a nap. I could have fallen asleep even now, immediately. I turned around and eyed the empty gallery. Empty, except a single woman, who had just taken a seat at the back raw. Who is she? Hair of uncertain color, with blond highlights, tied back in into a ponytail; face—hard to describe; dressed in one of those ugly suites favored by professional American woman—hers was black. She must be the defendant, the surgeon, I thought. Does not resemble the picture I remembered from the website but, I figured out, this is who she is. You cannot have a malpractice case without the accused doctor. I was expecting to see the defended surgeon sitting at her counsels' desk. But she decided otherwise; she chose, and was permitted it seemed, to look at the proceeding from far above—as if she were a bystander, a spectator—not the main actor of the play.

I looked at her and smiled. She avoided an eye contact. She knows who I am, she hates me, I thought. Understandably.

9:00. The Bailiff entered through the door at the back of the bench. "All rise. The court of Biloxi in now in session. Judge Baristheaut presiding."

The Judge sauntered onto the bench. A tall, heavy man. Around sixty, gray hair receding. Pudgy face. A black gown hiding a bulging paunch. With a grunt, he collapsed into his huge throne, assuming a semi-supine position. Legs spread out.

"Please be sited", said the Bailiff and retreated to his permanent position against the wall.

"Good morning, ladies and gentlemen," the Judge proceeded in a gruff voice, "calling the case of Katrina Gospel versus the Adventist Medical Center and Dr. Katlyn Conway. Are both sides ready?"

"Yes, your honor, we are ready." Both the senior partner and the children choir conductor jumped to their feet like obedient children.

"Mr. Furrer, you wished to make a statement?"

"Yes your honor." The short defense attorney rose up, walk to the podium and gave a ten-minute homily, explaining why the plaintiff's expert cannot serve as an expert in this case. Because, he is not an expert at all —he does not perform the procedure involved in this case and he does not use the tools used by the accused surgeon.

Again? Didn't the Judge already rejected their previous motion? I did not even bother listening to what he was saying. Who cares, whatever. Stay cool.

The Judge replied. I discerned impatience in his voice: "Mr. Furrer, we have discussed this before. Motion denied. Mr. Browning, your expert is accepted by this court."

Browning jumped to his feet. "Thank you your honor. He is already here", he pointed at my direction.

"Very well, you can call now on the defendant."

As the Dr. Katlyn Conway walked down the aisle of the gallery, I took notice of her sensible but expensive looking black, patent leather shoes, clicking on the floor. She crossed the bar and climbed on the witness stand. Like a little princess entering the court, ascending the throne to be coroneted, I thought. She was sworn in.

The senior partner gathered his notes and stood at the podium opposite her. I remembered that it was Veronica who had taken the surgeon's deposition. I hoped Browning had read the transcript thoroughly; he should be much harder on the surgeon than Veronica had been. My headache reappeared and I felt jittery, I found it difficult to concentrate. Besides, I was already absorbed with my own imminent appearance.

Browning started very gently. After the usual preliminary questions, he focused on the operation.

"So you inserted the Veress needle in the right upper quadrant?"

"Yes Sir. This is where I always insert it".

"Do you know about the Palmer point"?

"Uh huh".

"Yes or no?"

"Yes Sir, I heard people talking about. At a meeting…."

"Could you please tell us what is the Palmer point?"

"Well, some people prefer inserting the Veress on the other side, you know, here", she pointed to her left upper quadrant.

From his elevated pulpit, the Judge smiled kindly down on the witness. "Doctor, the court recorder cannot transcribe what your hands show. Please verbalize all your answers." Interesting face, I thought, central European, Hungarian?

"Thanks your honor. I'll do. I meant the left upper quadrant," said Dr. Conway.

Mr. Browning continued examining the surgeon: "Doctor, so you inserted the Veress needle in the right upper quadrant. Can you tell us what happened then?"

"Yes sir. It read occluded."

"What does it mean 'occluded', doctor?"

"It means that the monitor, the monitor of the insufflating machine, sensed that no air, I mean no gas was flowing within the tube…into the Veress needle…and the patient."

"And Doctor, tell us why the gas was not flowing?"

"Sir, I said that the system was occluded…because the needle most likely was not in the correct space."

"Not in the correct space, not in the correct place? And what would be the correct place doctor?'

"Sir, the correct place would be the peritoneal cavity."

"So where was the needle? Where was it if it was not within the peritoneal space?"

"Well, Sir, it could be anywhere. It could be situated under the skin, the abdominal wall, the muscle, the omentum. Anywhere".

"Could it be situated in the liver, doctor?"

"Very unlikely, Sir".

"Very well doctor. But please tell me, is there any way to confirm, I mean are there any tests available to help the surgeon confirm the correct placement of needle into the peritoneal space—where is should be, right? I mean, before connecting it to the tubing, er, to the CO_2 machine?"

"Yes Sir. There are tests. But all tests described are not reliable and most people do not use them."

"Do you know, doctor, about the saline injection and aspiration test or the saline drop test? Are they not accurate?"

"Oh yes. I know what you are talking about but experienced laparoscopic surgeons do not need any of those tests. We know how to insert safely the needle without any confirmatory test."

"Please explain, doctor".

The surgeon explained patiently—like a teacher talking to a retarded pupil—about the structure and function of the Veress needle: the blunt tip, the sharp end, the spring mechanism—how she can sense the 'click' when the needle penetrates the fascia into the peritoneum.

"But in this case the needle was not in the correct place, right?" asked the lawyer.

"Yes Sir. It wasn't."

"So what did you do next?"

"Well, Sir, I re-inserted the Veress needle?"

"At the same place?"

"At the right upper quadrant but not at the same place."

"What do you mean? Did you insert the needle through another skin incision? "

"No Sir. I used the same incision but directed the needle in a different direction. Different angle, you know."

"This is not mentioned in your operative note, doctor."

"Sir, not everything is noted in the operative report. Surgeons do not include each and every minute detail of the operation in the report."

"Okay Doctor. So what happened next? Did the monitor read 'occluded' yet again?"

"Yes Sir."

"And what did you do then, doctor?"

"I removed the needle and tested that it is patent, I injected saline through it. It was patent."

"And, doctor, what did you think at that stage? Why was the monitor reading 'occluded'?"

"Oh, we discussed it just a minute ago…it was not in the correct place." She is staring to lose her patience, I thought. Browning is doing well; if he continues this way, she may lose her Prima-Dona-like cool. Let her become a little emotional.

"You mean not in the peritoneal cavity? In the muscle? In the omentum?"

"Yes, yes."

"Okay, doctor. So next you have re-inserted the needle at the same spot, the third time…"

"No, not the same spot…."

The Judge: "Doctor, please let the counsel finish his question."

"Yes your honor. Sorry," replied the surgeon. Now she looked a little flustered to me.

"Thanks your honor," the senior partner bowed lightly to the Judge and addressed the surgeon: "I was asking whether you inserted the needle, now the third time, into the same spot in the right upper abdomen?"

"Not at all. I changed again the angle of insertion, the direction of the needle."

"It is mentioned in the op notes?"

"I told you already that the operative notes serve as an outline of what was done. An outline—not every detail has to be included."

"Okay doctor. Did you think at this point to do any test to confirm the correct placement of the needle?"

"No, no, no—nobody uses those tests…".

"Yes, I understand doctor. But did you think about changing tactics. For example, to use the Palmer point, we just talked about it? Or use an open access? Do you ever use the open access?"

"Rarely, in patients who had previous operations resulting in scaring, but this was not the case..."

"Thanks you doctor, I understand.“

Browning continued questioning the surgeon calmly and respectfully: "So you re-inserted the needle at the same place the third time…"

"No," she interrupted him, "I told you, I changed direction."

"Yes, I understand, but it was inserted at the same incision, now the third time?"

"Yes Sir," the surgeon finally conceded.

"And now the monitor read '20', what did it tell you? What were you concerns?"

"Well, I thought that we are not in the correct place, again."

"What did the pressure of 20 indicate? Could it be that the needle was located within a large vein? A large vein in the liver?"

"Hum, it could be…many things could be, it could have been anywhere. You know, in surgery not everything is black and white. There are many gray areas. Uncertainties."

"Uncertainties? Of course, but a pressure of 20 suggests a pressure within an abdominal vein during inspiration. Would you agree doctor?"

"Maybe, perhaps, it could be but we are never sure. It could be anywhere." She seemed to me a little agitated.

"So what happened then? Doctor?"

"Immediately after the monitor read 20 the patient's blood pressure dropped and her heart arrested. We started CPR."

"And what about the needle, doctor? You left it in the abdomen connected to the flowing gas?"

"No, no. I removed it immediately. I took it out!"

"Immediately, doctor? How soon? How long was the needle connected to the machine pumping gas into this patient's vein?"

"I told you that I removed it immediately. And we do not know whether the needle went into a vein…we will never know."

"But the patient sustained air emboli, so the gas must have been going into a vein, right, doctor?"

"No. There are other mechanisms for air emboli."

"Such as, doctor?"

"Well, CO_2 can diffuse into the venous system through the tissues, and, and there are other mechanisms."

"Right doctor. We will return to the topic of air embolism. You said that you removed the needle immediately but there is no mention on how immediate this was in the operative report. True?"

The surgeon appeared exasperated—how many times did she tell him that the operative notes do not have to describe everything. She did not reply.

"Doctor, please reply to the counsel's question," the Judge admonished her.

"Yes Sir, "she replied to the lawyer: "I didn't mention in the operative notes that the needle was removed immediately. Could I get some water, please?" The court clerk hopped up and handed her a glass of water.

Mr. Browning pushed on: "Doctor, do you know what is the Durant position? Why it's recommended in patient suffering from air emboli?"

"Oh yes, Sir, yes. It's the left lateral decubitus position, it's used to prevent air which entered the blood system from traveling to the brain."

"Thanks you Doctor. When this patient developed cardiac arrest, when CPR was underway, did you place the patient in such position?"

"Not initially. Only at a later stage."

"Again, this is not mentioned in your operative report…please tell me at what stage—how many minutes after the patient arrested was she placed in the Durant position?"

"I don't remember. Perhaps ten minutes, perhaps twenty minutes. You know what is CPR? Have you ever attended a CPR in the OR?—there are many people, anesthetists, nurses, internists, lab technicians—hard to remember details. Many things are happening at the same time. Everybody trying to save the patient. Really—no one has the time to count minutes and to record at what time precisely this or other thing were done." Conway seems to like talking. The more she says the more confident she sounds, I thought.

And so the examination of the surgeon by the plaintiff's counsel went on, lasting an hour. "I have no further questions to the doctor, your honor," declared Browning.

The Judge declared a recess and disappeared behind the door leading to his chambers.

The surgeon remained sitting on the witness stand, sipping her water. She seemed relaxed and happy, knowing that— whatever the outcome—her worst hour is over. I thought that Browning had started well but gradually lost momentum. Like a boxer, he managed to hit her lightly here and there, but there was no knock out—no definitive attempt to expose her negligence. I was surprised that the senior partner did not utilize snippets from the surgeon's deposition by Veronica. For instance: when she had made that ridiculous claim that it was not her who produced the air emboli, but it's the surgery itself to be blamed. Wouldn't it be interesting to see her confronted with what she had said then?

The Judge returned, collapsed into his chair and gestured the procedures to continue. Mr. Furrer sprang up to examine the surgeon. His job, obviously, was to paint Conway in the most favorable colors. It turned out to be a protracted, immensely dull and banal conversation between the two, lasting over an hour. The narrative of this chat between the surgeon and her lawyer must have been well rehearsed between the two—at least so it sounded to me.

The first quarter of the interrogation served to let us see that the surgeon is a "nice local girl" —born, raised and educated along the Gulf of Mexico—in brief, an "All Southern Girl" or a "Southern Belle" (i.e. "a stock character representing a young woman of the American Deep South's upper socioeconomic class."). Next, we were subjected to the story of her superb undergraduate and medical education in a series of leading local institutions. Obviously, of course, she had been trained in surgery in some centers of excellence under not a few surgical

giants. Surely, one of her teachers during residency was a famed
pioneer of advanced laparoscopic surgery. Following surgical
training she stayed for a year or two as a junior faculty ("I was an
assistant professor") but academia was not her call—"I wanted to
serve the community." So she'd returned to the Gulf and joined a
surgical practice in a medium size community hospital ("I always
wanted to come back to the ocean"). And let the audience not
forget that her husband is a leading neurosurgeon surgeon at the
same institution—aren't we proud to have both of them living
along us and saving our lives!

The following act consisted of the lawyer-surgeon *duet*
playing out yet again the story of the operation. Point by point—
step by step—everything of course was perfect and within the
standard of care—"this is what I was trained to do, this is what
my colleagues do". At this point, Conway appeared to be
enjoying herself: confident, articulate. To a chance observer
wandering into the courtroom Conway would seem and sound
like a professional woman interviewing for a higher positon rather
than a physician sued for malpractice.

Next act: Mr. Furrer wheeling in a large plastic anatomical
model of a human—the multi-color viscera showing under the
skin. "Doctor, please demonstrate to us where exactly you have
inserted the Veress needle?"

The surgeon, smiling broadly, replies: "I placed it here,"
pointing three cm' below the right subcostal margin.

"And Doctor, what structures, what organs are situated at this
site, can you point them to us?"

"Sure, liver, intestine, colon…".

"Now doctor, could you please point out the organs situated
on the other side—I mean the left upper quadrant. "

"Of course, here are the spleen and again the small bowel and
the colon."

"So doctor, was there any rationale to prefer the left side—
the…the Palmer point they call it, right? It's Palmer point?"

"Yes, it is." A big smile. "No, I don't see any advantage for
using the Palmer point over the right upper quadrant. This is what
you wanted to ask, right?"

"Thank you doctor."

Mr. Furrer went on. The Judge seemed slumbering in his
huge chair. I must have snoozed occasionally as well. Finally,

arriving at the point in time where the patient had arrested Mr. Furrer asked:

"Doctor, why didn't you place her immediately in the left lateral decubitus position?"

"Oh, we were conducting CPR, like in ACLS protocol, you know. Heart massage, ventilation, drugs. Can you imagine doing CPR with a patient hanging on her left side? Of course not. First comes the CPR—this is live saving."

"Thank you doctor," the counsel smiled victoriously towards the defense table. "I have no more questions, your honor." So, this is their new punch line of defense, I thought,— that the patient couldn't be placed immediately in the left lateral decubitus positioned because it would have interfered with the cardiopulmonary resuscitation. *Surely one could continue effective cardiac compressions with the patient on her side.*

Mr. Browning was now permitted to rise again, to ask a few questions, including: "Doctor, do you know Dr. Timothy Hutchinson in person? "

"Yes, Sir, we never worked at the same place simultaneously but I had the honor of meeting him. At meetings, symposia, I have even attended one of his courses, you know."

"Doctor, you must be aware that Dr. Hutchinson is the expert witness on behalf of your defense. Actually, he's scheduled to take the stand here later this week. Did you have any direct contact with him recently?"

"No Sir. Of course not." On Conway's expression I read: "Why do you ask me such stupid questions?"

"Your honor, I have no more questions to the defendant," said Dwight Browning.

The Judge suppressed a yawn and stood up.

"All rise," piped up the court clerk, "court stands in recess."

The surgeon stepped down from the stand, crossed the bar and walked up the aisle of the gallery towards the back door. As she passed me, I noted her self-satisfied smile. I guessed how she must have been feeling: like somebody who cannot swim, thrown into the middle of a lake, then realizing that the water is shallow—she can touch the ground with her feet. *They have been easy on her. Much too easy.*

The courtroom emptied rapidly. Veronica turned back towards me: "Coming to lunch with us?"

"Sure." I still felt lousy. I hoped that some food in my stomach could revive me.

The senior partner and his paralegal climbed up the steps. Down, at the defense table, the black plaintiff remained sitting alone, as if glued to her chair.

"What about her?" I asked. Isn't she having lunch?"

"Oh'," Veronica shrugged, "I think Katrina has brought something in her bag. I left her some water."

The café was just a block away but the legal team decided to drive. The senior partner offered me a ride in a brand new V-12 monster pickup. Much bigger than mine, I thought, probably he uses it to schlep his yacht. His Benz must be resting at home. Veronica joined the paralegal in the latter's small red BMW.

"A nice BMW," I said to Browning, "you must be paying well your paralegal."

"It's her husband's. An attractive girl, eh? Did you see her legs?"

Obviously, I had noted already the paralegal's endless, well-shaped legs, on high heels, below her colorful "Gone with the wind" sort of a dress.

At the lunch joint, each member of the legal team ordered an outsized sandwich. I got a bowl of chowder soup, which I consumed, understandably, with little appetite. The legal team nibbled on their food, ignoring the large portion of side fries. We drank water, although, I thought, some wine or beer could be beneficial before climbing on the stand. I remembered what the late Professor Boris Savchuk used to preach—that the best remedy for hangover is cold beer. Early mornings in Moscow, after long vodka-filled nights, he would stop his Volvo at little roadside kiosks. Drink, drink, Mark, nu, drink, *davai*, he would hand me a beer. Not here, I thought sadly, Browning would freak out if I order one.

We chewed in silence. To break the oppressive hush I asked a few questions. "So what's the story, how many times that Furrer is planning to object to my credentials or expertise, or lack of it?"

The senior partner smeared more catchup and mustard on his sandwich. Veronica replied: "You know, the hospital has a very strong management and an influential board of trusties. They are very proud of their hospital and doctors, their reputation. The couple, the surgeon and her husband, the brain surgeon, are tremendously respected in the community. They will do anything to defend them. Money is not an issue for them."

"And what about the Judge? In the absence of a Jury, he's the sole arbitrator, right? Is he a fair guy, do you know him?"

The senior partner pushed away his plate. "Of course we know old Leslie Baristheaut. He has been practicing law around here for years, before elected a Judge in 2009. At some point, he even was a prosecutor. But we have to go back to court now." He stood up, looked at me with a sardonic smile and said, "Doctor, the term 'fair' doesn't exist when it comes to litigation. The truth at trial is always subjective!"

Back in the pickup, burning half a gallon of fuel to cross half a mile, I asked, "I see that you want to be a Judge. Right? When's the election?"

Browning looked at me coolly. "Oh', I'm working on it." We kept silent the rest of the drive.

That was the last direct interaction I had with that great litigator of New Orleans.

19

"Please stand. Raise your right hand. Do you promise that the testimony you shall give in the case now before this court shall be the truth, the whole truth, and nothing but the truth, so help you God?"

"I do."

"Please state your first and last name." I give my name.

At this time of the day, I would be rather napping at the side of the hotel's pool. After lunch is my snooze time. Back at the hospital, I use to lie down on my office carpet for a power-nap of 15 minutes. But here I'm on the stand of the court house of Biloxi getting ready for whatever would come next. The two *ibuprofens* I swallowed in the toilets just before entering the courtroom are dissolving in the stomach. *What a nasty and prolonged hangover.*

I look down. Veronica is gathering her notes. The senior partner is scribbling something. Is he working on another case? The plaintiff is still sitting at the same spot. Her expression blank as before—the air emboli apparently had damaged her cortex. Did she eat her lunch? They could have given her a few bucks to buy something. Up, up at the top of the gallery I see Dr. Conway. Now she is a spectator. From now on, to the end of the trial, she will sit up there, watching the opera played out according to the script that she had written on that fateful day in the OR. She sang soprano. Would my tenor be adequate to negate her claims of innocence? Or would Dr. Hutchinson's bass prevail?

"Mrs. Chapman, please proceed", the Judge orders. He seems in good cheers. Probably had a satisfying lunch. A glass of vino?

The junior partner approaches the podium.

The next forty-five minutes goes on smoothly—as expected. After a series of preliminary, background questions she comes to the point:

"Doctor, are you an expert in the field of abdominal wall hernias?"

"Of course I'm."

"Are you an expert in doing operations such as that performed by the defendant on Mrs. Gospel, namely, an umbilical hernia repair"?

"I am. I have been doing umbilical hernia repairs for thirty-five years. I do that operation at least every month, if not every week. But I use a different technique."

"Thank you doctor. And are you an expert in laparoscopic surgery?"

"I am. I have been doing laparoscopic surgery for some twenty-five years. However, I prefer not to use laparoscopy for umbilical hernia repairs."

"Why is this doctor?"

"I don't find laparoscopic umbilical hernia repair to be advantageous. In fact, I believe that the opposite is true."

"Doctor, can you please tell us the definition of the "standard of care'?"

I do.

"Great. And according to that definition, do you believe that the defendant in this case adhered to the standard of care?"

"No, I don't think so."

"So based on your expertise, do you believe that the standard of care was breached by the defendant?"

"Oh' yes."

Over the next few minutes I try to make the point that while the initial insertion of the Veress needle in the right upper quadrant was not a breach of the standard of care, and that not doing any "confirmatory tests" after the first insertion was sort of "OK", the obstinate persistence of doing it again and again at the same site—not changing the tactics—not stopping and thinking—not trying the Palmer's point, or even an open access, was a breach of the standard of care. I add: "I discussed this case, of course without disclosing demographic details, with many surgeons around this country and abroad. I did not get even a single opinion supporting the surgeon's practice in this case."

"Objection!" The defense lawyer jumps to his feet, "this is hearsay."

"Sustained", says the Judge, "doctor, you cannot tell us what other people told you."

Next Veronica leads me through the events that took place after the third attempt of the needle's insertion. "Doctor, could you please explain to the court what is the Durant position and why was it so important to use it immediately after the patient suffered cardiac arrest?"

"Objection!" The children-chorus-conductor springs up again, "she's leading the witness."

"Overruled," decides the Judge. "Please proceed but try not to put words in the mouth of the witness," he adds benevolently, probably realizing how inexperience Veronica must be.

The answer is ready in my mouth: "So, most likely the Veress needle was inserted into a hepatic vein, a vein inside the liver. As I have already said, the pressure of 20 recorded by the insufflating machine is typical of a pressure within an abdominal vein during the inspiration phase. The machine pumped CO_2 gas into the vein and from there the gas travelled into the patient's heart. Reaching the right side of the heart... the right ventricle, the gas formed a "lock"—a large bubble—which blocked the outflow of blood from the heart to the lungs. This is what caused this patient's arrest. At this stage, placing the patient in left lateral position—with her right side up—would move the air lock away from the ventricle's outlet because, you know, the air tends to float upwards. When the outlet is open, blood can pass into the lungs, and from there into the left heart, and the rest of the body, and the patient recovers her circulation. This obviously is a lifesaving maneuver. "

I sense that Veronica is happy with my elaborate reply; she keeps nodding her head and looking at me enthusiastically. Then she asks: "Is it your opinion, doctor, that not placing the patient immediately in the left lateral decubitus position was a breach of the standard of care."

"Yes I think so. And by the way, there are clinical reports published in the literature of patients suffering from air emboli during laparoscopic procedures and immediately recovering their circulation after being placed in that position." I am tempted to add that one of those articles has been authored by Dr. Hutchinson but decide against doing so.

"Objection," shouts the defense counsel, "no such publications has been disclosed."

"Sustained" The Judge agrees with the defense.

"Thank you your honor. I have no more questions to the witness." Veronica returns to her chair.

Mr. Furrer stands up, making himself ready for the cross-examination. I remind myself to take a few deep breaths. I think that the examination by Veronica went smoothly and restored my confidence. Even my hangover seems to abate gradually.

I stretch my legs under the table and relax my shoulders. Yes, I did fine, but until now, I was only under sporadic, friendly fire. Now I have to get ready to absorb the confederate's heavy artillery. I take a sip of water.

The defense lawyer places himself opposite my stand, his legs apart to gain stability.

"Doctor, thank you for coming down to the South. We appreciate it very much. I hope you enjoy the weather."

"Oh yes, thank you Sir." Just move on, I think, bring it on.

"Doctor, you said that you are the only surgeon in your little town, right?   How big is your town? What's the population? Two thousands? Three thousands?"

"Yes Sir. I live and practice in a small town but we serve the whole county, of about thirty thousands, perhaps more. And I'm employed by a large system which serves a significant portion of the State."

"But the population of the town is only a few thousands, right?"

"Yes."

Mr. Furrer smiles gently, his body language transmitting: This is a small town surgeon…what experience could he have…a hillbilly type of a surgeon trying to teach us what is right and what is wrong?

After more of the same, Mr. Furrer starts to focus on the operation.

"Doctor, you are not doing procedures like this performed on the plaintiff, right?"

"I do exactly the same procedures but not laparoscopically…not anymore…"

"In your deposition you said that you've attended a course on laparoscopic ventral hernia repairs, right? At Mount Sinai Hospital? When was that?"

"I think it was around 2000 or 2001."

"And you said that you decided not to perform such procedures in your practice, right".

"Yes, but…"

"So doctor, currently and at least over more than ten years you have not performed a procedure using the technique relevant to this case. Right?"

"But…"

"Doctor, yes or no?"

"Yes."

The defense lawyer turns around and grabs a small object from his table. "Your honor, can I approach the witness?" he asks the Judge.

The Judge nods, "Yes."

Furrer hands me the small object. It is a disposable Veress needle. "Doctor, do you know what this is?"

"Yes, sure, this is a Veress needle. A disposable one."

"And please tell us when was the last time you've held such needle in your hand?"

"I stopped using Veress needles some twenty years ago," I reply, "instead, I'm using the open access…because…".

"Okay doctor, let us understand. You don't use the Veress needle—in fact you have never held a needle exactly like this one—which was used in this case-—because this is a disposable needle which was not available twenty years ago!"

"But, but, they are the same, disposable, no disposable, they are the same…" I try to interject but Furrer does not allow me. "… and you don't do laparoscopic umbilical hernia repairs. Is that correct?"

"Yes but I have to mention…"

"Doctor is that correct? Yes or not?"

"Yes," I admit. He will not let me have a chance to elaborate. My anger is mounting.

Now the defense lawyer addresses the Judge: "Your honor, for the record I would like to mention that the witness has no personal experience with the operation performed on the plaintiff and with the instruments that were used."

"I hear you Mr. Furrer. You made this statement before. Please don't repeat yourself," the Judge drawled laconically. "Please proceed."

I look down at "our" legal team. Their faces are blank. Veronica is scribbling something. I look up to check how's our Southern Belle—the accused surgeon—doing. She must be having good time, I think, enjoying the aria.

The defense lawyer fiddles for a minute or two with an overhead projector. "Your honor, I hope this projector works." He places a transparency on the projector.

"Doctor, do you recognize this?" he asks me, pointing to the image projected on the wall.

Fuck! I predict what would come next. Let him work hard on this item, I am not going to help the bastard.

"Not really," I reply.

"Doctor, you don't recognize the list of chapters from your memoir?"

"Well, it's not the complete list…"

"But this is your memoir, right?

"You can call it so if you like."

For the next hour, Furrer brings up numerous bits and pieces from the memoir—anything which could portray me as a chronic problem maker or a psychopath.

"Doctor, in South Africa, was it in Johannesburg, you had a shouting match with the director of Surgery…Professor Becker? "

"'Yes, we had some disagreements from time to time but later he promoted me as his deputy. We were good friends…"

"Doctor, did you break at night into the Chairman's of Surgery personal office and stole your personal file?"

"Not exactly…"

"But this is how it is described in your memoir. You wrote it. Yes or no?"

"I did write it."

"Doctor, in Haifa, Israel, you walked, armed with your military assault rifle, into the department of surgery and threatened your director, the chief of surgery Professor Maccabi. Right?"

"This is inaccurate. I did not threat anyone with a rifle. I had the rifle with me because I returned directly from military reserve duty. We had an argument…and by the way, this is not his real name…".

"And he fired you, right?"

"I was not fired. My contract expired."

"But the director of the hospital did not wish to renew it…".

"You can distort my life story as much as you wish…"

"Doctor, yes or not?"

I am silent. How should I play it out? When will the senior or the junior partner interfere? Why didn't they warn me in advance about such blitz?

The Judge looks down at me: "Doctor, you have to answer."

"Yes," I say, "whatever."

The defense lawyer appears satisfied. Like a fly, I am now caught in his cobweb. He is an experience spider, I think.

"Doctor," he continues, "in New York, in Brooklyn, you fought with the other surgeons in the hospital, accusing them to belong to a so called "Irani Mafia". True?"

"Yes, and I was on the right side, I won. This has been documented in the New York Times…"

"But you were fired…"

"I was not fired. Didn't you ask me the same question at the deposition? I told you that I was offered a golden parachute, and I took it. I could have stayed on if I wished."

"And then you moved to a hospital in Bronx, where you invented yet another mafia—now you called it the Indian Mafia, right".

"This is ridiculous", I reply, "you are taking scraps and fragments from what I wrote for fun some ten years ago, distorting events and facts, taking it out of context. You are completely distorting my life story. Ridiculous." I had enough!

Furrer pauses. Half a smirk is painted on his face. As an experienced orchestra conductor—that he is—he awaits patiently for the Judge to sound his trombone. And the latter admonishes me gravely: "Doctor, you cannot use such language in this court. If you do, I'll have to expel you."

I stay silent.

Furrer continues with increasing vigor and enthusiasm. "You called them an Indian Mafia because they didn't refer patients to you…"

The Judge does not let him finish the sentence. He explodes: "Mafia, mafia…I don't need to hear anything about any mafia anymore. I get your point, Mr. Furrer…it will be included in my deliberations…but now," the Judge moves his hand like a farmer guiding his hen back into the coop, "just get on with the case. Just move on. Mafia…" He sneers.

The defense lawyer appears unmoved by the Judge's admonition. "Doctor, after you were fired from the Bronx Hospital…".

"I wasn't fired. I was fed up and decided to move on…."

"OK, after you were forced to leave that hospital…"

"I was not forced to do anything…". How long would this game continue, I ask myself. The Judge decides for us. "Let's take break," he says grumpily, "doctor, you remain under oath.

During the recess you are not allowed to talk to anyone." The
Judge disappears into his chambers.

20

I stepped down from the stand and walked towards the back door leading to the vending machine. I passed near the senior partner. His face was white. I heard him hissing sotto voce to Mr. Furrer: "Listen Francis, you overdid it, wait and see what I'll do to your witness tomorrow…". I could not hear the defense lawyer's reply. On my way out, I went by Dr. Conway—she was sitting at the same place, pretending I do not exist.

With a fresh bottle of water, I returned to the witness stand awaiting for the torment to continue. At this point, I lost interest in the proceeding. My only desire was to leave this court and jump into the hotel's swimming pool. Let them continue their game without me.

After a quarter of an hour or so—it felt much longer—the Judge returns. His face is red. Did he have another swig? Grisham would have made the Judge sip Jack Daniels from a flask hidden under his bench. *I could use a drop as well.* "Please continue," the Judge nods to Mr. Furrer.

"Doctor, after Bronx you moved to Iowa. A town called Fort Madison, right."

"Yes." I am self-aware that my tone and body language are now becoming hostile and impatience.

"You had a fight with the anesthetist in the OR. Her name was Dr. Indira?"

"This was the nickname I gave her. We had a clinical argument…"

"And did you head-butt your partner, Dr. Cappuccino?"

"You are wrong. This is not the real name of my ex-partner and I did not head-butt him."

"But you broke his nose, true?"

"If you say so…"

"Yes or no?"

"No. I did not break his nose," I reply. Furrer shrugs his shoulders.

"Doctor, did you author or co-author a book on complications in surgery?"

"Yes, I did", I confirm, relieved somewhat to change the topic, leaving behind my tortured memoir.

"In that book, did you classify complications, using the terms…" Furrer looks up at the Judge and adds in an apologetic tone, "your honor, I'm embarrassed using such term in court but I'm quoting directly from the witness' book." He looks at me: "Doctor did you describe complications using the terms 'shit happens'?"

"Yes but you are taking it out of perspective…"

"Your honor, 'shit happens', this is the level of this witness' professionalism!"

"Objection. The counsel is badgering the witness," the senior partner raises his voice. *Finally.*

"Sustained. "Mr. Furrer," says the Judge, "I understand the point you wish to make. But we had enough of this. Let's take a five minute recess. The witness," he looks at me," is not allowed to speak with anyone."

I remain put. I look at my watch: almost two hours on the stand.

The Judge returns. *Is his prostate enlarged?* Mr. Furrer re-positions himself behind the podium. His curt grin unchanged.

"Doctor, in your memoir you wrote that you have missed what you called the 'laparoscopic revolution'. That having to change places, the years you moved from South Africa to Israel, and from Israel to this country, were wasted on political struggles and acclimatization and therefore you did not have the opportunity to become a laparoscopic surgeon. True?"

"What I meant was that I didn't have the opportunity to dedicate myself to advanced laparoscopy, meaning complex laparoscopic procedures like bariatric surgery…"

"Doctor, did you write this or not?"

"Yes, something along those lines but you're distorting it."

Furrer looks around the courtroom victoriously. Like Napoleon after the Battle of Austerlitz, I think.

"Doctor, would anybody be able to conduct an effective CPR, you know, cardiorespiratory resuscitation, with the patient lying on her left side?"

I reply: "Mr. Furrer, in this case, if the patient would have been immediately placed in left lateral decubitus position there would not be any need to continue the CPR. Anyway, you can compress effectively the chest of a patient in the lateral position.

The CPR does not unlock the gas lock from the atrium but the left lateral position does."

Furrer smirks: "So doctor, you would postpone the CPR?"

I start replying: "You will continue CPR on a dead patient if you don't unlock the ventricular outflow…" but the lawyer is not listening. He waves his hand as if I were an insect. His face expresses contempt: listen to the crap this idiot is talking.

"No more questions, your honor." Furrer returns to his chair along his hitherto silent partners.

The Judge looked at the defense team. "Mrs. Chapman?"

The junior partner rose. Will she give me a chance to explain? To redeem my professional life story?

An expert cannot simply lecture to the court. He has to be guided by his lawyers. He cannot boast about his own qualifications. Instead his lawyer should prompt him: "what are you academic qualifications, what books did you publish…why do you think that you are qualified to comment on the case even if you do not do lap hernia repairs…." But "our" team was passive—impassively sitting on their hands while I was being grilled for hours. Now they had a chance to stand up and clarify a few points—lead me into correcting my image—explain items.

Veronica had only one question. "Is there anything in your memoir that you are ashamed of? Anything that you now, in hindsight, would wish to hide?"

"No. All lives are complex and eventful. Mistakes are done. Some people write about it and some not. I am quite happy with my own life story. Thus, I hide nothing. "

"Thank you doctor. Your honor, this is all. I have no more questions for the witness."

"You may step down," the Judge said to me.

Even before I had the chance to vacate the witness stand, Francis Z. Furrer, III, was on his feet again. "Your honor. Can I make a statement?"

"Yes, but be short. A minute— not more!"

"Thank you your honor. Yet again, we wish to point out that the expert witness for the defense is not an expert in is field. Not only he has no adequate training in laparoscopic surgery but he has no idea about the procedure performed, and the tools used, on the plaintiff. Furthermore, his life story suggests a deranged personality that spent most of its professional career in futile and misguided skirmishes with his superiors and colleagues. One is left with an impression that he had no time to engage in actual surgical practice. Thank you, your honor."

My job done, I relocated to the visitors' gallery. The judge announced another recess following which the last witness of the day was called to testify. The man, some academic neuropsychologist, was hired by the defense to claim that the patient's post cardiac arrest mental deterioration should not be attributed to the prolonged brain ischemia but to her history of drug abuse.

I am not going to stay for this, I thought. I waited a minute or so: perhaps Veronica and Browning would have something to say to me? They did not turn around.

I grabbed my backpack and walked towards the back door. The 'Belle' was still sitting there, at the backrow, avoiding my eyes. I retrieved my cell phone and walked out pass the security. A southern winter evening was falling. I rushed to the casino, changed and, at last, jumped into the deserted swimming pool. Half an hour later, I immersed myself in the steaming whirlpool. The sun was setting down; cool breeze blowing from the ocean. I closed my eyes, feeling the slime being washed away from of my skin and brain.

21

In the evening after my 'martyrdom' at the court of Biloxi, I was half expecting a phone call from "our" lawyers. At least, I thought, Veronica would call to offer some explanation, reassurance—anything to comfort me that I did not screw up completely. There was no sign of life from the legal team.

To celebrate my last night in Biloxi I strolled to the French Old House, considered the leading eatery in town. I had read about this restaurant in Grisham's *The Runway jury:* "An old white building …a locally famous restaurant where most of the town's legal community usually gathered for lunch when court was in session."

The place was half deserted. I was not forced to sit at the bar but allowed at a table for two.

"What is your best seller?" I asked the black waiter.

"The stuffed snapper, sir".

I consulted the menu: "A lightly seasoned filet of snapper generously stuffed with our superb shrimp and crabmeat au gratin baked to perfection and accompanied by pasta topped with crawfish *etouffée*.

"Sounds yum, and a glass of Malbec please."

The fish was superb. Worth the trip, I thought. I finished the Malbec and declined another glass.

I settled the bill and left. Will I ever be paid by them, I asked myself. Will they reimburse me for my expenses and time? Many, if not most, expert witnesses would demand the money upfront—at least a fat "retainer". They are worried that if the case turns belly up the law firm may decide to "forget" paying the expert. I read somewhere on the internet that this is not such a rare phenomenon. Perhaps I was being naïve not asking for anything in advance before this trip?

Back in the casino hotel business went on as usual. A long line in front the 'eat as much as you can' restaurant; octogenarians in wheel chairs, drawing desperately on their cigarettes, or on their O_2 cylinders—pulling obsessively on the handles of the slot machines. At the bar—where else should I go?—another band was already playing. I noticed that the college girl is back, talking to two older obese men in colorful Bermuda shirts. I sat on a stool at the other side of the bar. Another whiskey and soda. This time I lit up a cigar—a medium-size Cuban—ignoring the "please no cigars" signs. I knew that the barman would not care—he did not.

It is all about the money, I thought while sipping slowly the second Scotch. Money and power, like in politics. Lawyers on both sides are playing a poker game—the harmed patient, the plaintiff—is just a lowly card. The defense team and the defendant(s) start the game with a better selection of cards: behind them, they have the all mighty insurance companies or self-insured hospitals, with unlimited resources. They hire top lawyers who in turn can buy top experts—money is not an issue. The plaintiff's legal team, on the other hand, works on a contingency basis; if they win, they get a third of the money but if they lose—as commonly they do—they get nothing. To win they must invest in a good card—the expert witness—but good cards are hard to find, can be costly and may fail. What about me? Was I a good card? Did I fail today? Yes, it is a Poker game but an interesting one, I thought, now the whiskey flowing in my brain: risky, painful but enjoyable.

"Another one?" the barman asked.

"No thanks. Let me have the bill please." I did not intend to repeat last night's binge.

I was trying to extinguish the stub of my cigar by drowning it in the ice melting at the bottom of my glass, when the college girl materialized at my side.

"Hi there."

"Hi." She looked differently tonight: short black leather skirt, tight black silk shirt, high heels, lots of make-up. A college girl no more.

She smiled at me: "Would you like to do something with me tonight? That is if you're in a better shape for doing something. Not like yesterday." She giggled. I noticed her large blue eyes. "But tonight you are going to pay," she added, now seriously.

She was tempting, she was appealing, but the illusion has evaporated and so did my libido, which from the start was inversely proportional to my added years.

I smiled back. "Thanks, not tonight. I'm a little tired, you know. But, actually, I'd like to ask you about last night. What happened? Who paid for your time?"

Her smile vanished. "These are things that I can't discuss. Anyway, I hope you enjoyed your day in court. Have a safe trip back home." With a wave, she stood up and moved to the remote corner of the bar.

She cannot be cheap, I thought. A thousand bucks per night? At least, if not much more than that. They must have hired her. Who are "they"? Furrer? Browning? Perhaps both shared the bill.

I slept well that night.

At 8:55 am, I was back at the courthouse of Biloxi. I had to catch an early afternoon flight but I did not want to miss the testimony by Dr. Timothy F. Hutchinson—the expert for the defense.

I seated myself on the left, at one of the top rows on the visitors' gallery. Dr. Conway arrived a few minutes later. I looked at her as she took the same seat as on the day prior, at the backrow on the right. This morning she changed into informal attire: a pair of designer blue jeans and a white blouse under a blue sport jacket; she wore her hair loosely open over the shoulders. *Much better.* Down below I saw the plaintiff, sitting, like yesterday, at the table with Browning and Veronica; she wore the same faded tracksuit.

Dr. Hutchinson climbed on the witness stand and was sworn without delay. Mr. Furrer positioned himself at the podium and begun the examination. Hutchinson looked exactly as I remembered him from a past surgical conference: tall, square faced, handsome, but older—his hair turning pre-maturely white. I thought that he has put on some weight. He wore a dark blue expensive looking pinstriped suit, a white shirt and a red silk tie. He had that classical look of a successful American senior politician or a movie star from the 1950's.

After letting the witness describe at length all his qualifications, positions and achievements in the world of surgery—including that he is the shining star in the field of laparoscopic hernia surgery—Furrer zoomed on the case under discussion.

"Dr. Hutchinson, do you believe that Dr. Conway has breached the standard of care in her treatment of Mrs. Katrina Gospel?"

"No Sir. Not at all. Nothing that Dr. Conway did could be considered as being outside the scope of the standard of care."

"Doctor, do you believe that Dr. Conway has erred by inserting the Veress needle in the right upper quadrant, not using the left upper quadrant, the so called Palmer point, as the insertion site?"

"No, Sir, I don't believe that she has committed any error. In fact, the SAGES manual, the manual published by the Society of American Gastrointestinal and Endoscopic Surgeons indicates that insertion of the Veress needle either on the right or the left upper quadrant is appropriate."

This is bullshit. I had consulted the manual: I knew that it mentions the right lower quadrant as an option—not the upper one. *Where is the manual?* Let him bring the manual and show us. Browning has to call him to task on this item during his cross-examination. But how do I make contact with Browning?

"Doctor Hutchinson," the defense lawyer continued, "do you believe that the defendant has erred by not doing any tests to confirm the correct placement of the Veress needle?"

While listening to the question, I walked down the aisle and sat just across the bar, a few feet away from Browning and Veronica. I placed my elbows over the bar, covered my mouth with my hand and whispered, "Veronica, Veronica." Then, louder, "Veronica, Veronica, pssss." The heads of both Veronica and Browning remained glued to the front, listening to the witness' reply:

""No, I don't believe that any such confirmation tests were indicated. There is no data to show that the saline test or aspiration test are appropriate tests to show that the Veress needle is in the right position. Typically, the surgeons I trained with, the surgeons I work with, and the surgeons I'm busy educating, don't perform these tests."

"Veronica, Mr. Browning," I hissed louder. Katrina Gospel turned her head towards me, her eyes expressionless, and then she turned it back. "Veronica," now louder.

Now Veronica could hear me. She looked at me with a question mark. With my hand, I signaled: "come towards me…we have to talk."

"Sir, Sir, the gentleman at the gallery. Please be seated. Please be silent. Or I will remove you from this courtroom," boomed the Judge from his bench.

I dropped back on my chair. I saw Browning looking at me with no interest, his face transmitting "what does he want?"

Veronica did a rotating movement with her index finger: "later, we'll talk later."

Well, I thought, didn't Browning say, "leave Hutchinson to me"? So let us see how he deals with him.

Meanwhile Hutchinson continued answering a question after question, politely, patiently and eloquently, each word in place, no hesitation—like a skilled TV presenter. "Yes," he said, "three attempt of needle insertion at the same time are OK. Only after the third attempt I would consider using another site." He stated that, "open surgical repair as suggested by the Plaintiff's expert would have a higher risk of complications." When asked about Dr. Conway's response and conduct after patient developed cardiac arrest Hutchinson said: "She did exactly what I would do: starting chest compression, CPR. Moving the patient to the left side position as suggested by Dr. Zohar would not be appropriate."

I watched him as he was saying this: none of his fascial muscles moved——a poker face. *A liar.*

The Furrer-Hutchinson dialogue did not need to last more than fifteen minutes to allow the expert justify everything Conway had done as appropriate, just perfect.

Now it was Browning's turn. His last and only chance to swing the pendulum of justice into our side.

Browning moved towards the podium with empty hands. He must have all the questions in his mind, I thought, or he does not intend asking many. I saw Hutchinson sitting calmly, smiling to himself, playing with a large wristwatch that he took off his wrist. In a few minutes, his job finished, he will hop into his car and drive back to his Hernia Clinic in northern Florida, half a day drive. Or he could fly from New Orleans. Or maybe, I was thinking, he'll decide to stay another night at the casino hotel, gambling with the small fortune paid him for his lies. Who knows—they may even offer him the same "college girl".

Browning's cross-examination did not last longer than ten minutes. He addressed the surgeon cordially. No one entering the courtroom at this stage would be able to decipher on which side the lawyer asking the question is—on the defense side or the plaintiff's one. I realized immediately that Browning would not challenge the expert with any of his previous publications, which had offered opinions contradicting what the expert was stating today. *Leave Hutchinson to me* Browning had promised and look what he is doing now. *Why?* Didn't I warn "our" legal team that Hutch is a big fish and a formidable opponent and recommended tactics to use against him?

A few brief questions by Browning, a few longer statements by Hutchinson:

"Sir, had Dr. Conway followed the recommendations of the plaintiff's expert when Mrs. Gospel became asystolic, Mrs. Gospel would have died due to the CO_2 emboli."

"No, Sir, I am not aware that chest compressions are possible and effective if performed in patents in a lateral position."

"Sir, we have to realize that what happened to Mrs. Gospel was a rare complication."

"I have no doubt that Dr. Conway efforts on behalf of the patient was extraordinary. I have no doubt, Sir, that Mrs. Gospel received outstanding care."

I ran down the steps of courthouse even before Hutchinson stepped down from the witness stand. It was like walking out a Broadway play before it ends. I walked to the casino hotel, gathered up my things and asked one of the Valet boys for my Silverado, handing him five bucks.

I took the coastal highway back to New Orleans. On the radio, an evangelical preacher was constantly ranting against some Satan. I changed the station. A politician was raving about candidate Trump. I switched him off.

I was replaying in my mind the 36 hours in Biloxi. Veronica, Browning, Furrer, Hutchinson, the Judge, the Plaintiff, Dr. Conway and, yes, even the "college girl". *What do I know about them, their inner lives, their motives?* In my mind, they were portrayed as stereotypical characters. If anyone would want to re-write this little saga into a brief Grisham-like legal novel then the characters would have to become multidimensional. Being familiar with so many surgical personalities, I could recreate a believable Conway and Hutchinson characters but what about the others, the Judge for example? What did I know about him and judges in general? I even could not guess how he would judge on this case. And the character of the narrator of the story, myself—should it not be further developed?

I dropped off the pickup at the airport. I landed in
Minneapolis. Driving home through the familiar, snowy northern
woods soothed my mind.

A few weeks later, I received an e-mail from Veronica:
"Do not be disappointed in anything—your testimony for the
Plaintiff was exactly what it needed to be. As far as Mr. Furrer's
questioning, we made our objections, but the Court ruled he could
continue his questioning—the outcome was beyond our control.
As to Dr. Hutchinson, he did what he was hired to do—defend
Dr. Conway. His testimony was not a surprise. Your expert
opinion has been very much appreciated throughout this process."
A nice girl, Vernonica..

Part 5: THE JUDGEMENT

22

The Judge, snubbing the clichéd proverb, "Justice Delayed is Justice Denied", took almost a year to pen the seven pages of double spaced text of his Judgment.

Veronica predicated the delay in an e-mail:

"It will be a long time before the Judge rules. We had another case in front of the same judge that went to trial two years ago and we still have not received the judge's ruling on that case. He has to write an opinion, and the Court is backed up with other rulings and opinions, so it takes time."

How fresh are the events of the case in the Judge's mind when, a year later, he finally decides to write the verdict? I asked myself. By then, he must have had been sitting on numerous cases: the images of lawyers, experts, plaintiffs, defendants, probably blurred and confused with each other, or nonexistent. He has to rely solely on the transcript prepared by the court recorder. As if we surgeons would decide on the fate of our patients based on what has been written in some old notes, ignoring the facts gathered during a recent face-to-face encounter. Now contrast this with a verdict by a Jury: they see, they listen, they feel and they vote on the verdict in real time.

Eleven months after the trial Veronica wrote:

"We lost the case. The judge ruled in favor of the defendant and that there had not been a breach in the standard of care committed by Dr. Conway or the hospital. We are not going to appeal."

I read the Judgement.

It opened with a few lines under the subtitle "Findings of fact":

"...the procedure was aborted, chest compressions were initiated, echography documented CO_2 emboli...patient was placed in left lateral decubitus position...". Nothing about the time line, nothing about the delay, nothing about the damage inflicted to the patient.

136

The next page was titled "Testimony of Dr. Katlyn Conway": a brief summary of what the surgeon had told the court.

The following sections were dedicated to the two experts' testimonies—and the way it had been worded pre-shadowed the Judge's decision.

The Judge devoted many lines to diminish the statue of the Plaintiff's expert—no word about his past achievements and qualifications: "Dr. Mark Zohar is not board certified in any field, including laparoscopic surgery, because he did not performed his residency in the USA"; "he has not used the Veress needle in the past 20 years…and has limited experience with laparoscopic hernia repair…this diminish his credibility as an expert in this case…he failed to objectively articulate the standard of care to which general surgeon performing an umbilical laparoscopic hernia repair by a Veress needle is held," and, "additionally, he failed to casually connect the purported breach of the standard of care to a particular injury that Mrs. Gospel received."

Really? So the air emboli were the act of God?

Dr. Hutchinson's testimony received a different treatment: a detailed outline of his glorious training and career, and a long list of surgical societies to which the witness belongs, including the American College of Surgeons. As if, I thought, I do not belong to the latter or other societies. What followed was exactly what Hutchinson had said in court: everything was faultless; extraordinary efforts by D. Conway..."

The Judge concluded:
"The Plaintiff bears the burden of proving, by a preponderance of the evidence, that the Defendant was liable in a medical malpractice action. The trial judge, sitting in a bench trial as the trier of fact, has the sole authority for determining the credibility of the witnesses. Therefore, it is the trial judge's prerogative to give weight or credibility to one witness testimony versus the other..."

"The plaintiff's expert has limited experience with laparoscopic hernia repair and the use of Veress needle and that diminishes his credibility as an expert in this case. The defendant's expert had the greater training, experience, and credibility. It is therefore ORDERED AND ADJUDGED that the

Adventist Medical Center was not negligent, and Dr. Katlyn
Conway did not breach the standard of care."

I e-mailed Veronica:
"This seems a text book case on how to defend successfully a
clear case of surgical negligence: hire a local top guru expert for
the defense, smear the plaintiff's expert, find a biased judge and
omit a jury."

Veronica replied:
"Do not take it personally. As you know, Mississippi is a
very conservative jurisdiction and Harrison County is one of the
more conservative areas of the State. It is very, very difficult to
win cases for the injured patient there".

This did not satisfy me; I had to discuss it further. I called
veronica:
"I appreciate your mail but please tell me: if it is so hard to
win a case for an injured patient in Harrison County, Mississippi,
was there any point to invest resources into this case?"
"We do our best doctor."
"Yes, I know, but once the defense had nominated Dr.
Hutchinson as their expert I sensed that we will have hard time. I
didn't know that the case would be conducted without a Jury and
that defense will attempt to harshly assassinate my character and
expertise."
"I understand doctor, but this is how such games are played
out."
"But couldn't you guys have played is better? For example,
your senior partner could have predicted the narrative of this court
case and its outcome..."
"We did all what we could, doctor."
"I know, but listen: so after my deposition, you guys could
have perceived that pitting me against Dr. Hutchinson in front of
a Mississippi Judge, in a small Mississippi town, without a Jury—
is like pitting Bernie Sanders against Donald Trump in front of
the citizen of Biloxi. You could have decided to drop me and find
a more suitable expert, somebody more locally attractive, yes, I
know it is hard to find, or you could have aborted the case. Hallo,
are you still there?"
"I'm listening doctor."

"Well, I got the impression that your senior partner had little interest in this case, you know, a low cap on potential rewards, and had little hope to win it. I guess that he takes on, occasionally, a hopeless case, in order to look good in the community—the big compassionate lawyer taking on cases of poor blacks. Something he can talk about in the Yacht Club. Like 'we tried to help that poor black woman…pro bono…'".

Silence on the other side.

I went on: "Besides, anyone who wants to be elected a Supreme Court judge would want to get a few black votes, right?"

"Doctor, unfortunately Mr. Browning lost the election last month."

Epilogue

23

I never heard again from Veronica, Browning or Furrer. I guess they continue to do what they think they are good at: suing doctors or defending them. Dr. Hutchinson? A while ago, I read about him in the New York Times: he was nominated to the position of the Secretary of Health in Trump's administration. He did not get the job. Probably, he continues repairing hernias, travelling around the world, teaching others how to do it.

And Mrs. Katrina Gospel? Our poor, old, fat, black woman, whom we saw sitting silently, starring into the void? Well, who cares about her? Nobody. She was left with severe brain injury, and without a cent in compensation. Justice Mississippi style.

Over the years, I was involved with a decent number of surgical legal cases. This was the first case that I have ever supported that has been "lost", that I did not succeed helping the legal team to obtain some compensation for the harmed patient. However, this is how stories can end in the real Biloxi—unlike the ones in Grisham's books.